T0197098

TRAIL OF THE EAGLES

R.S. HASPIEL

authorHOUSE®

AuthorHouse™
1663 Liberty Drive
Bloomington, IN 47403
www.authorhouse.com
Phone: 1 (800) 839-8640

Published by AuthorHouse 01/31/2018

ISBN: 978-1-5462-2729-8 (sc)
ISBN: 978-1-5462-2730-4 (hc)
ISBN: 978-1-5462-2731-1 (e)

Library of Congress Control Number: 2018901416

Print information available on the last page.

For LoElla Marie Gramlich, in memoriam.
She was my friend and partner of 13 years
and without her love of South Dakota
this book would not have been written.

Contents

Chapter One

Highway 212 — The Road Home

Highway 212, north of Rapid City and heading east across the South Dakota prairie is one of the most desolate stretches of road to be found. Shells of old Nike missile silos dot the side of the road for miles. All that remains now are the square fenced plots of land, sometimes with metal pipes protruding from what were, during the Cold War, the nation's nuclear launch pads. The silos, built in the mid-fifties and early sixties, each contained a missile outfitted with a nuclear weapon and prepared for launch by the Strategic Air Command in Omaha. Now cattle and sheep graze around the silos, much the same as they had when the sites were fully loaded with nuclear bombs.

During the Cold War, it was mandatory for high school seniors in the area to complete a Civil Defense course. They were taught the measurement of Roentgens, levels of radioactivity, half-life, and survival strategies. The government probably believed they were protecting folks from the very real potential of nuclear disaster, but not many of the residents in this sparsely populated ranchland ever took the threat very seriously. They simply weren't aware that they were ground zero in the event of a nuclear attack. New York or Washington, maybe, they thought, but not the middle of Dakota.

West River Country, as the rolling grasslands west of the Missouri River are known to locals, is much the same as it has been for the last fifty years. Kathryn knew this because she was raised here, and like most of her generation, fled the area in search of a better life in the cities. Some classmates, after becoming disillusioned by the congestion and pace of city life, returned to manage family farms and ranches, but most stayed in the cities, established careers, and were integrated into urban cultures. She followed the path of the latter, graduating medical school in the late '70s and entering the field of scientific research at the University of Miami Medical Center. As she sped down Highway 212, she reflected on her journey, knowing that she was coming home again to a place that was familiar yet as distant as those memories of the past.

"Dammit", Kate yelled as her foot crushed the brakes, sending the Jeep Cherokee into a skid. The deer continued its dash across the road and into the sweet clover on the left of the road. "How could I have forgotten the danger of driving at dusk here," she thought. Broken windshields and numerous road kills were common along 212, especially when driving at sunset or after dark. All locals knew this, like city people knew not to drive through certain neighborhoods at night. Almost a tribal instinct of knowing your surroundings and unconsciously responding to them. These instincts never really disappear. Her eyes now quickly scanned the roadside for the bright glimmer of eyes reflecting off the headlights. Having rediscovered prairie driving skills, Kathryn returned to thoughts about why she had been summoned back to South Dakota, and why the Bureau of Indian Affairs requested the services of an independent forensic investigator rather than a government expert. She had no unique expertise that wasn't available through government resources, and a close childhood friendship with BIA staffer, John Redbull didn't seem reason enough for the request.

On April 6, her office at the University of Miami received a call from a John Redbull of the Cheyenne Indian Reservation. He was seeking the whereabouts of Dr. Kathryn Stafford and asked that she contact him immediately. When Kate's secretary gave her the message, she immediately speculated that only a family tragedy or class reunion would generate a call from someone who she hadn't spoken with in over twenty years. She hadn't expected John's contact to be related to work.

"Kate, we need your help," he said after a brief recap of their lives over the past two decades. "We have a bit of a mystery out here, and I think you may be able to help solve it. It's very important that this be kept quiet for now. No one needs to know what we've come across until I've got some explanation about what we're dealing with. You know the bureaucracy, tell them you can't solve the crime and they bring in truckload of government experts and the FBI. That's the last thing I want to deal with now."

"Sounds serious, John. What exactly is it that you think I can help you with?" she said, still unsure of why he was briefing her on what clearly sounded like Federal government turf.

"Kate, here's the situation, last fall a sheepherder name of Wes Johnson was herding out on Sam Rassmussen's place, actually running sheep on rented Indian land along the Cheyenne River. He never came back. They found the sheep and his trailer, but no sign of him. Three days ago, a couple of Indian kids found him at the entrance of a cave, dead since last winter we think. He was pretty well preserved, as its just now beginning to thaw out here. Anyway, Kate, he didn't die of natural causes. Somebody killed him, crushed his skull, cut him down the middle and threw him in that cave. My people are afraid someone is going to accuse an Indian, since it happened on Indian land. Kate, I know nobody here did it! Nobody had reason to. I need to get some idea of who did it and why before the authorities are notified. I figure if he's been on ice all winter, a while longer won't hurt anybody. That's why we need you. We need to find out how he was killed and if there is any evidence that would lead to the killer. Will you help us?"

"You know I would help you if I could, John, but this sounds way out of line for me; first, I'm in Florida and second, there are just a few ethical questions about how this is being handled. Promise me you won't get yourself in serious legal trouble!" She could only think of how routinely and professionally this would have been handled in Dade County. Autopsy, coroner's report, police report, investigated, and then probably filed away like so many other homicides of the unknowns.

"Kathryn, this is South Dakota, remember? It's a reservation issue so we don't have to get Pierre involved. And the death certificate we can file any time. I just don't want to see the FBI out here again, and I don't want my people accused of something they didn't do. I don't think the tribal counsel here at Eagle Butte will put up with the tactics the Feds used down at Pine Ridge. And I don't want them to go through that kind of investigation and false accusations. These are simple people, certainly not agitators and murderers."

Kathryn knew he was referring to the Wounded Knee affair of the late '70s when the FBI stormed the Pine Ridge Reservation, arresting members of the American Indian Movement and terrorizing the local population. After that incident, tribal authorities for all South Dakota reservations attempted to maintain a low profile, hoping to protect the local people from similar Federal intervention.

"But if you can't help, you can't. I just thought you were the only one with professional knowledge who I knew and could trust. We're prepared to pay you well, you know," John pleaded. "But if you can't, you can't. I'm sure you keep pretty busy with all that crime down in Miami. I hear they're killing somebody every day down there."

"Oh God," she thought. This reminded Kate of the time long ago when John coerced her into jumping off the barn roof and onto the hayrack. He was ten and she was seven. He told her that only she could save the kittens from being bound inside a haybale. If she was too frightened to jump, the kittens might die. The little girl believed him and jumped to save the kittens. While the kittens were rescued, her ankle cracked in the process, still an injury Kathryn was reminded of when jogging.

"Yes, they do keep me pretty busy here. Miami isn't the murder capital they make it out to be, but we do have more than our share of crime," she replied thinking how curious it was that, like John's reflection on the differences between cultures on the Cheyenne and Pine Ridge Indian reservations, the diversity in Miami was much the same — a melting pot of people sharing common geography but vastly different values. Some were radicals, while most were peaceful citizens, seeking stability for their families and a share of America's prosperity.

"Look, John, give me some time on this. Can I call you back tomorrow after I've given it some thought. If I can't help you, maybe I can offer some advise."

"Sure, Kate," he replied pensively, "but don't hold me up for too long. I have to do something soon."

Three days later, Kathryn Stafford found herself behind the wheel of a rented 4-wheel drive Jeep, propelling over the washboard asphalt of Highway 212. As she watched the distant lights from the town of Faith come closer, she thought about her connection to this land and its people. It felt good to be home.

Chapter Two

Homecoming

She opened her eyes to the site of a small knotty pine room and the sound of an eighteen wheeler, gearing up so as to blast through her door, or so it seemed. The old oil stove in the corner tried its best to growl out heat, but it was losing the battle with a strong northwest wind that penetrated the walls. She pulled the comforter tight around her neck and surveyed the room for evidence of a coffee pot. Nothing. April in this north country vacillated from spring-like warmth to deep winter cold, and always at night, the temperature dropped below freezing. Her watch said 9:30, 7:30 Mountain time. Time for this Floridian to face the cold if she were to meet John Redbull in Dupree by 10:00.

Today Kathryn dressed in jeans and boots and slipped on her old leather bomber jacket with the soft sheepskin collar. As the door opened, a blast of wind hit her face and whistled against her ears. The Cherokee's windshield was singed with frost. How anyone could or wanted to tolerate the long, severe winters here was a mystery to Kate, yet she, too, had lived in it a long time ago.

Faith's main street consisted of the indoor plaza with grocery store, cafe, and other basic necessities at the north end of town; the requisite bars, hardware store and grain elevator to the south. A few pickup trucks dotted the street, with most of the town's activity centered at the restaurant. As Kate walked through the door she smelled the toast and coffee and listened to the familiar Midwestern twang as ranchers and townspeople sat around stainless steel tables catching up on the local news. Harry's boy got a job in the oil field over in Wyoming, and the wrinkled old cowboy at the counter is going to pick up some replacement heifers at the sale today.

"What can I get for ya?" inquired the fuzzy haired waitress in pointed glasses perched on a face prematurely wrinkled by years of dry air and Dakota winds.

"Just a cup of coffee and some wheat toast", Kathryn replied, aware that most of the men in the cafe glanced briefly her way, then returned to their conversation.

"Are you here for the sale?" asked the waitress sloshing weak water-like coffee into her cup. Monday was sale day at the cattle auction in Faith.

"No, just passing through to Dupree," she answered, glancing at the coffee made white by the cream she had added. She made a mental note to buy a coffee pot, thermos, and a strong Colombian blend when she settled in at Dupree. She never understood why Midwesterners drank their coffee about half the strength of people on either coast.

If Faith, population 900, is a small town, Dupree is a spec on the road. However, it is the county seat of Ziebach County and location of the Bureau of Indian Affairs office run by John Redbull. Tribal headquarters were 60 miles east in Eagle Butte, but John's office handled administrative affairs for the local area. Dupree was reputed to be a local hotbed in the early '90s when the local tribe confiscated businesses in town, claiming rights to cafe, liquor store, and a few other key establishments as Indian property. Local store owners and surrounding ranchers fought to retain the property and a deepening wedge was drawn between whites and Indians in the community. These events probably made a good case for John Redbull's efforts to keep the murder of the white sheepherder a secret. Kate still wasn't sure were she stood on the local issues. It wasn't necessary to take sides if you didn't live in the area. Now, she thought, she was in a position of supporting the tribe, no matter how she felt about local issues. She hoped that this wouldn't present difficulties in completing her work here.

As Kathryn pulled her truck into an open spot in front of the brickfaced building identified as B.I.A. offices, she recognized the familiar stride of a tall, lanky man approaching the building. John Redbull stood 6'1", with straight black hair and the high cheekbones of an Oglala Souix. Unlike the walk of most native Americans who exhibited a more gliding, easy gait, his stride was long and purposeful, And most notably, unlike most Indians whose eyes are piercing dark brown, John's eyes were a quiet blue-gray. But John Redbull was most definitely full-blooded Oglala and proud of his family and heritage. John graduated from the University of South Dakota in the early seventies, majoring in Business Administration. He returned home to work with his tribe, and like so many young adults of the time, was committed to improving the lives of his people. He had stayed here on the reservation, working in an atmosphere of poverty, alcoholism, and hopelessness that remained a stigma of reservation life. Given the opportunity to advance to a Washington post with the Bureau, he chose to remain in the local office. He believed that most real change took place at the grassroots level and his most important role as a leader was as an implementer rather than policy maker.

Kathryn stepped out of the truck and opened the back door. As she leaned into back seat to retrieve her briefcase, a soft voice from directly behind questioned, "Kate?"

"John, I knew that was you coming down the street, I would have recognized that walk anywhere," she said as she turned to look up at the tall frame. She reached up to hug him. He smiled, put his hand on her head, and tousled her hair.

"You haven't changed a bit, still a gangling girl in boots with long legs," he said laughing, but with a look of relief in his eyes. "I'm so glad you're here. Are you hungry? Want something to eat or some coffee?"

"Coffee would be great. Have some in your office?", Kate asked, still hoping that there might be a decent cup of coffee somewhere in the state.

"Yup, right this way."

The remainder of the day, the two sat over hot coffee and a stack of files, clippings, and photos of events leading to up to the discovery of Wesley Johnson's body. As John had indicated in their phone conversations, photographs of the body showed it was reasonably in tact despite the length of its repose in the cave. After surveying the files, Kathryn realized that there was little information to go on and that a full forensic investigation would be required. From sketchy reports on the disappearance of Johnson, it would appear that he had been dead for about five months. Since sheepherders are often in distant pastures for a month or more, no one knew exactly how long he had been missing. It was only when the stock owner realized that Johnson's return was long overdue and the severe winter weather was setting in that someone went to look for him. They found the sheep some four miles from Johnson's camp. His horse had been found earlier by a neighboring rancher. It had drifted into their pasture, saddled and uncared for in early November. The rancher reported that he had tried to locate the owner but was unsuccessful. He had put the horse in his pasture, believing that someone might claim it in the spring.

From all reports the sheepherder had been a loner, attracted to the job because it paid a decent wage and allowed him the freedom to roam the remote land, far from civilization. People said he was good with animals, loved horses and sheep, and would spend hours tracking and watching wildlife. He had no relatives in the area, and was thought of as a drifter. One report indicated that his drivers license gave Ekalaka, Montana as his last address. So it wasn't too surprising that no one initiated an active search when it was finally discovered that he was missing. It was still somewhat alarming to Kathryn, however, that a man missing for five months, who had left his horse and his trailer with all of his belongings, was not missed. A police report had been filed, but interviews with his employer and those in the area who knew him rationalized his disappearance to his own eccentricity. A man with no friends and little contact with the outside world might decide to leave the area with no trace. Wesley Johnson, evidently, was that kind of man.

Kate stood up from the table where she had been sitting for over six hours, let her glasses fall from her face, and stared out the window. "It looks like we have a lot of cracks to fill in these files, my friend," she said. "I've prepared an agenda, and there are number of arrangements that need to be made. I hope you don't mind being my gopher for a lot of this."

"Of course I don't mind. Anything you need, we'll get it.

I'm afraid your working conditions may not be what your used to, but we'll do our best. I've arranged for you to stay at a small house just off Main. You should be comfortable there. You have access to a telephone and I'll arrange for a Fax machine at the house.

"Good, I'm compiling a list of things I think we'll need as well as a number of interviews and site inspections. I want to examine the body, of course, but I also want to inspect the location where the body was found, the victim's trailer, and his horse. We need to interview the boys who found him and the rancher who has the horse. Also I want to speak to Johnson's boss and anyone else who knew him." As she spoke she also activated a small tape recorder for the notes that she would transcribe to her laptop that evening.

"Now, I'll take you over to the house so you can get settled, and then you're coming home with me for supper. Nancy is expecting you, and my oldest son will probably drive you nuts with questions about Miami and police investigating work. Just tell him to go away when you've had enough."

John had met his wife, Nancy, while they were in college. They were perfectly suited to one another. While John was quiet and pensive much of the time, Nancy was more outgoing and spontanious. Her social skills enabled her relate well with almost everyone, from the most downtrodden Indian on the reservation to the Washington officials who visited occasionally. She often worked with John, and as a team, they had done much to improve the lives of many on the Cheyenne Reservation. At home, Nancy and John were devoted to their family and both enjoyed horseback riding and camping and fishing. Their oldest child, Margaret, was a sophomore at South Dakota State, and their son, John Jr., or JR as he was called, still lived at home. The boy was undecided about his future, and John wished that he would soon find direction in his life. He had hoped that Kathryn's visit might help JR find that focus.

The small house off main street was spartan, but comfortable; an entryway for coats and boots and a door leading to the small kitchen. A kitchen table, countertop, gas stove, a relic refrigerator, and yes, a coffee maker and toaster on the counter. To the left of the kitchen was the living room, and beyond it, two bedrooms and a bath. The living room was comfortably arranged, a small fireplace centered on the wall and a gas stove in the corner. Next to the stove was a large desk facing the window, and a sofa against the back wall centered below a large print of an Indian scout and horse atop a prairie hill. The house was warm and offered privacy for Kathryn to work.

After a filling supper prepared by Nancy and John, they talked about old times and caught up on the important events in their lives since Kate had last visited. JR was fascinated by Kathryn, and as John had warned, was filled with questions about forensics and Miami. Kate promised to let him work with them on the investigation. She hoped his father didn't object, but seeing how enthused the boy was about investigative work, she hoped it might motivate him.

By 9:30, Kathryn said her good-byes, and thanking them for the wonderful supper, returned to her cottage. The fireplace and sofa looked inviting. She stacked kindling and newspaper on the fire grate, topped it with small logs from the woodbox, and watched as the tiny flame grew larger. She then unpacked her laptop, plugged in the adapter, and nestled into the sofa. How peaceful it is here, she thought, so far away from the intrusions of the city. Only the crackle of the fire and the dancing motion of the flames reflecting on the walls. "Civilization can keep its distance tonight", she thought, "what a shame to screw up this perfect scene with sounds of 'You Have New Mail'." She switched off the laptop and placed it on the floor beside her.

Chapter Three

The Investigation

When Kathryn Stafford awoke the next morning, she felt totally rested and refreshed. Morning rays of sunshine spread dust sheets across the room and she could still smell the residue of smoke from the fireplace. As she sat down at the desk and drew back the curtains from the window, she realized that she would need to call her office in a few hours to brief them on the evidence she would probably be sending them for inspection and analysis. After careful consideration of the investigation she was about to initiate, Kathryn felt strongly that several legal and ethical decisions must be made at the onset of the project. She knew that after a cursory inspection of the body, the coroner must be notified and an official autopsy performed. She also knew that once notification had been made, an official investigation would be set in motion. If her timing was right, as it had been many times before, her sleuthing efforts would be well under way before the Federal and local bureaucracies had settled their jurisdictional issues. Often in Florida, it took days, often weeks, before turf issues were resolved, and Kathryn had learned to use this time to her advantage when initiating her forensic work. It was her nature to be more interested in solving the crime than in achieving notoriety for it. She derived satisfaction from using her professional skills and inquisitive mind to achieve results, and while it may have detracted from her political advancement as a forensic investigator, she never wanted the spotlight. Those in her profession knew and respected her capabilities, and it was recognition from her peers that held importance and value.

Modern day forensic investigation utilizes a broad range of scientific, medical, and computer technologies in addition to investigative methodology and psychopathology. A good investigator uses every tool available, but continues to rely on a sixth sense based on intuitive curiosity and personal observation. Like a puzzle, each piece of evidence plays a specific role in identifying what took place. Even lack of evidence in a specific area, holes in the puzzle, help to reconstruct the crime. Missing pieces also have a story to tell.

Today's investigative teams are comprised of pathologists, psychopathologists, forensic accountants, forensic examiners, engineers, biochemists, geologists, and computer scientists. This bevy of multi-disciplined experts approach crime investigation from many perspectives, combining each specialized effort to establish a profile of the crime, victim, and perpetrator. Those professionals with expertise in conducting on-site investigations and evidence collection have a unique set of skills. They know what is important, and how the results of each individual discipline influences the outcome of the investigation. A good on-site forensic investigator will orchestrate the use of each piece of evidence and every investigative procedure to solve the crime. Kathryn Stafford was known for her experience in this area.

Kathryn decided to walk to the local cafe for breakfast. It would give her an opportunity to listen in on the gossip and re-orient herself to the culture. Besides, a plate filled with bacon, eggs, and fried potatoes would stick with her through the long day ahead.

Amid the clatter of dishes and sound of voices speaking in both English and Indian dialect, she eased on to a stool at the counter. As she glanced around the room she saw a few faces that were familiar, but couldn't attach names to them. From the table in the corner, an old man in a green Pendleton shirt stared at her, then got up to approach the counter. "Didn't you grow up around here", he asked, "Stafford's girl?"

"Kate Stafford," she replied, searching for a name to connect to the weathered face.

"I'm Tom Crowfeather. I knew your father. He was a good man, used to bring us coal from up north. I haven't seen you since you were a little girl. Where do you live now?"

"Good to see a familiar face, Tom. I'm here visiting from Miami. I live there now. How have you been? Do you still live south of town?" She now recognized him, and remembered when she rode with her father to bring coal and other winter supplies to Indian families in the area. Tom's ranch had been one of her favorite stops. She loved playing with his animals. There were dogs, chickens, ponies, and lambs in his barn yard, but also, there was an assortment of wild creatures that Crowfeather rescued from time to time. She recalled the pet antelope that ran to her when she arrived, the black and white skunk who thought he was a cat, and the orphaned baby owl. Tom had introduced her to each of the animals, as if they were one of his family. And before she and her father departed, he had always presented her with a toy he that had made.

"I still live on the place," he replied. "They want me to move to town, think I'm too old to be out there by myself. But I don't want to live in town, too much noise and too many people. Besides, I got my horses and nobody there to take care of them."

"I remember your ranch," she said fondly. "I loved to play with your animals and you would give me toys that you had made. My dad said you had good horses, the best around." It suddenly occurred to her that if she were to inspect the sites where Wesley Johnson herded sheep and where the body was found, she would need a good, surefooted horse. "Tom, do you suppose you might have a horse I could ride while I'm here? I would be happy to pay."

"Sure, I have a good horse for you, Tennessee Walker with a real nice gait. Real tame, too. I don't want your money. You just come out to the place and get her. I know," he said with a smile and twinkling eye, "you come home to do rodeo, ride those barrels? This isn't a good barrel horse, just chases cows."

"Afraid my barrel racing days are over, my old friend," she shyly replied. "I just want to ride up in the hills, like the old days. I really appreciate your lending me the horse, and I'll take good care of it. I'll be over in a day or two to get her."

With a good ranch breakfast and the promise of a horse to ride,

Kathryn left the cafe in search of a topographical map and the locations of the people and sites she wanted to investigate. Clearly, today's priority would be an evaluation of the existing evidence, particularly the body of the victim.

Wesley Johnson's body was stored in the cooler at the local meat storage plant. Tuesday night he was transported to the medical facility in Eagle Butte. Dr. Kathryn Stafford, Dr. James Eagan, John Redbull, and his son JR were present for the delivery of the body and its subsequent autopsy. Kate had determined that immediately following her noninvasive examination, the body would be turned over to the resident coroner for a full autopsy. His report would enable her to formulate an investigative plan.

Kate began an inspection of the victim's clothing and personal belongings. The jeans were soiled with wear marks on the back of the legs and seat of the pants. This, she assumed had occurred when the body had been dragged from its original location to the cave. The shirt had been ripped open in front with tear marks, cuts, and missing buttons. On closer observation, however, the tears appeared to have been initiated from above a body already lying down, more of a pull from top to bottom. The victim had no jewelry and no wallet. Among his belongings, however, was a walking cane. The engraving on the side said "Faith Livestock Auction Market, Faith, SD." His boots were worn and soiled, with chunks of dirt at the heal and around the sole seams. She searched each pocket of the jeans and shirt, finding a few cents change, a whistle, a ball-point pen, and a small black canister containing an exposed roll of 35mm film. How out of character, she thought, for a sheepherder to have 35mm film on him. She made a mental note to search for a camera among his possessions, but now she wanted to see what was on this film. She carefully bagged the evidence along with notations. The shirt, pants, and boots would be examined for hair, fiber, tissue, blood, and soil samples. This evidence, along with hair, fingernail, blood, and tissue samples would be sent to the lab for analysis.

Late that evening, the preliminary autopsy report was completed. Wesley Johnson died from a massive brain hemorrhage caused by a blow to the back of the skull. The rather large object used in the attack had collapsed the back of the skull, leaving bone fragments and brain tissue exposed. The incision made in the abdominal cavity was made after death. The cut was made with a scalpel-like instrument. Among bone fragments found in the cranial region, the pathologist also discovered a piece of rock material, possibly a portion of the weapon used to strike Johnson. This small sample, along with the other specimens would be sent to University of Miami labs for forensic testing. The 35mm film would be developed locally. Kathryn placed the film in an envelope. She would dust the canister for finger prints tonight and send it with John's son, JR, to Rapid City for processing in the morning.

As the Jeep crested the final hill approaching Dupree, she could see town lights in the distance. Kathryn was tired. There was still work to be done, however, and a lab would need to be set up at the house to perform at least minimal tests. Tomorrow marked the beginning of her site investigations, and she would need more physical stamina than was typically required in urban forensic research. Miles of horseback riding and rock climbing weren't part of the typical routine in Miami, but in Western South Dakota it was part of the job.

Wednesday morning, Kate awoke to the aroma of coffee. Sunlight entered from the window across the room, and she sluggishly rolled her body from the bed and padded toward the kitchen. Overnight, the kitchen had been transformed into a makeshift laboratory. Microscope, ink, notepads, and specimen glass covered the counter. As she reached for a clean cup, the phone rang.

"Dr. Stafford, this is JR. My dad said you need me to go to Rapid for you this morning. I'm ready to go whenever your ready."

"Thanks, JR," she replied. "Why don't you come over in about 15 minutes and I'll have the package ready for you."

Tossing on a sweatshirt and clean jeans, Kate wiped the film canister and placed it in an envelope. She would instruct JR to find a reputable processor and wait for the film to be developed.

By the time John and JR arrived, Kathryn had packed a bag with supplies for the day's work. They would be visiting the ranch where the riderless horse had appeared, and she hoped that the horse would provide some clues.

Chapter Four

Sam Pickens

John's pickup lurched as the wheels thumped over a cattle guard that marked the entrance to Sam Picken's ranch. The wrought iron sign overhead said Flying W Ranch, Home of Fine Appaloosas. A dirt road wound its way to the bottom of the hill where Kathryn could make out the figures of several men loading horses into a large trailer. As John pulled his truck up next to the trailer, a short stocky man in his mid-forties, sporting a black Stetson and alligator boots strolled up to the passenger's window.

"Hey, John, good to see you," he said smiling. "What brings you out to these parts? No Indian business out here that I know of."

"Good to see you too, Sam. I'd like to introduce you to Kate Stafford. She's doing some work for us and would like to ask you a few questions about the horse you found here last winter."

"Well, I sure don't know what this pretty lady wants to know about that ol' horse. He's not much of a horse but if you're interested in him I 'spose we could work out a deal," Sam said in a drawl that could only come from Texas or maybe Oklahoma.

"Oh, I'm not interested in buying the horse," she replied. "But I would like to ask you a few questions about how it strayed onto your ranch, and I'd like to look at the horse and saddle and anything else that was on him."

"Well now, I'd sure like to help you, but it don't look like no Indian horse, no brand on it or anything. Say, this wouldn't be anything about that sheepherder kid, would it? I've heard some stories around that they found him dead up in the hills. Know anything about that, John?

John quickly replied, "I can't say for sure that the rumor is true, but we think there might be a connection between him and that horse, and it would be a help if we could look at him."

Sam backed a step away from the pickup, as if to gather his thoughts. "I sure don't think its connected, but it was about the time he was missing. Tell you what, young lady, I'm awful busy here right now, got to go load some heifers we just bought. Leaning forward to Kathryn's window, he added, "Why don't I meet you in town tonight, and I'll tell you everything I know about the horse. About 7:00 at the City Club? In the mean time, you go down to the barn and see Tim. He'll show you the tack and you can see the horse in the pasture if you can catch him. Pretty wild in the spring, ya know. Might be hard to even get close to him. But help yourself."

There was something about the smirk on his face that made Kathryn feel like he was playing a game with her and would enjoy seeing her running through his pasture after the elusive horse. She couldn't help but think that this middle-aged "awe-shucks" cowpoke would be less than forthright in his efforts to be helpful. She also detected a nervousness in his body movements as he turned on the charm. Nonetheless, she needed information, knew damn well how to catch a horse, and knew Pickens could provide her with details as to time and place of the sheepherder's disappearance.

She reached into her coat pocket, pulled out a card and wrote a number on it. "Here is my name and phone number, Sam. Please call if there is any change in plans. I'll meet you at the restaurant at 7:00."

Sam put the card in his shirt pocket as he leaned into the truck. "John, you go down and talk to Tim. He'll show you around. And young lady, I'll see you tonight."

As they drove toward the barn, John snickered, "Well, he sure seemed to like you. I thought he might be in heat!"

"Please, I'm not looking for a cowboy Romeo! He probably doesn't have a clue as to what I'm looking for or why I'm here. Then again, maybe he does. I'm not real comfortable with the man."

"Then I'm coming with you tonight. If you don't trust him, then I should be there to make sure you're OK. He won't try anything with me around."

"Hey, big brother," she said laughing as she punched him in the shoulder, "I'm a big girl now from the big city. Promise, I can handle him. Besides John, it's not necessarily my honor I'm worried about. There's something about that man that's a little slippery, and I intend to do some digging to see what's under the good ol' boy front. It's all part of the job, a part I do fairly well, I might add."

Looking at her with a concerned smile, John replied, "Well, that's what your here for girl. You know what your doing. But I'm here if you need me."

As he stepped out of the truck a walked toward the barn, John too had questions about Sam Pickens. Where did Sam get the information about the sheepherder's body, and why did he appear to also connect the stray horse to that man? And, why hadn't the rancher questioned the BIA's involvement in the investigation? Indian Affairs typically didn't get involved in local law enforcement unless an Indian was involved, yet Sam didn't seem surprised at his inquiry.

"Tim?" John questioned as they walked toward the young man cleaning a horse stall. "I'm John Redbull and this is Kathryn Stafford. Sam told us you could show us the saddle that was on the horse that strayed in here last fall. We'd also like to see the horse."

"Oh, sure," said the boy. "The saddle's over here. Not much of a saddle. Just cleaned out the saddle bags 'cause they were stinking. There was an old sandwich in there that I threw out."

"Find anything else in there?" Kate asked.

"Ya, just some old stuff that's still in there.

Kate and John inspected the saddle. It was well worn, old, probably from the thirties or forties. Someone had attached leather padding to the seat to make it more comfortable for long rides. The length of the stirrups were set for long legs, indicating a tall rider, and the leather tie straps were worn showing considerable use for carrying ropes and other supplies. Kate handed John a pair of rubber gloves for use in inspecting the saddle and contents. The contents of the bags were of particular interest. In the first bag they found a screw driver, small pair of sheepsheers, a buck knife, a tube of grease, and work gloves. The second bag contained personal items: a tube of lip protectant, pencils, a small notebook, and a small sketch pad. Kate opened the sketch pad and paged through several drawings of wildlife and prairie scenes. Not bad, she thought. Whoever owned the saddle had talent. The notebook contained random lists, a grocery list, supplies, itemized expenses, and what appeared to be herd counts and lambing dates. There was little doubt in her mind that the saddle belonged to someone who worked with sheep, and although it was too soon to make a definite connection to the victim, this piece of the puzzle seemed to fit. She took the liberty of bagging the notebook and sketch pad, and laid the rest of the contents on a workbench. Taking a digital camera from her bag, she photographed each piece, the saddle and saddle bags. She then inventoried the contents and placed them back in the saddlebags.

"Well, lets go find a horse," John said. "Tim can you lend us a bucket of oats and a halter and point us in the right direction?"

"Better than that, sir", the boy responded. "I'll take you to him. There's a lot of horses in that pasture so I need to find your horse. He's the only bay so he shouldn't be too hard to find."

They drove the truck through a shallow crossing of the river, and Kathryn could hear the rustling sound of cottonwood trees in the wind and the call of a redwinged blackbird nestled in the cat tails. She gazed out at the bluffs across the river and felt a rush of old familiarity with the land. A sudden sense of peace and balance was with her. She could feel her heart rate slow while her senses came alive — listening to the prairie, smelling the water and sweet grass, watching an antelope dart up the side of the river bank. Oh, how she had missed these sensations. "God," she thought, "has preserved this solitude, and it remains here for those of us lucky enough to come across it." She had found some solitude in the Everglades and on her boat in the Keys. They were a welcome release from the sensory overload of the city. But nothing compared to this. At that moment, she made a commitment to herself to build a cabin out here, and to use it as her private hideaway.

Jolted back to consciousness by the thud of a protruding rock hitting the underbody of the truck, Kate spotted a small herd of horses grazing on the side of the hill.

"There he is, over to the left," said Tim. "Looks like he's got a limp."

The horse still had its thick brown winter coat, and as it slowly moved to reach a new clump of grass it was obvious that it favored its right hind leg. The three wranglers quietly got out of the pickup and gathered rope, oats bucket, and halter. Each person spread out so as to form a half circle as they walked softly toward the horse.

"Here, boy, quiet now," whispered Tim. "Want some oats, easy boy, quiet now."

The horse lifted his head, and with a soft snort, surveyed the situation. The sound of shuffling oats in the bucket got his attention as he cautiously moved toward the boy.

"Hand me the rope real easy," Tim whispered. As the horse sniffed the bucket and then lowered his head to munch the oats, Tim gently ran his hand along the horses neck. As the horse lifted its head, Tim calmly slipped the rope over him, gradually tightening the loop. "Good boy, your a nice boy." With that, the horse resumed eating and John and Kathryn gently approached him with the same quiet chant of "Easy boy, good boy." Kathryn slowly moved her hand down the right side of the horse's body, scratching him softly and watching for signs of fright. But the Bay seemed comfortable with the attention and rubbed his head against her shoulder. Once the halter was in place they could lead the horse back to the ranch where they would inspect his leg and overall condition. Kate swung her legs into the truck bed and secured the lead rope to the side.

Once back at the corral, John lifted the horse's hind foot to inspect the hoof and leg. The horse had been shod, unusual for a saddle horse in these parts. There generally was no need for horseshoes unless the animal was ridden over long distances or on hard surfaces. The hoof had grown far over the size of the horseshoe, but on closer inspection John discovered that it wasn't the excess growth causing the pain. Lodged in between the shoe and the back left side of the hoof was a two-inch long sliver of bone or rock. With a pliers, Tim removed the nails and shoe to find that the quick of the hoof was severely bruised by the object. "Looks like this has been wedged in there for a long time," he observed as he handed the object to Kate, then continued to remove the remaining shoes. Kate swished the sliver in water as she removed the dirt from its edges. This didn't exactly look like bone and it didn't exactly look like a rock. Suddenly she made two simultaneous deductions: first, the piece closely resembled the material removed from the skull wound of the victim, and second, it looked surprisingly like a fossil fragment! That the two pieces from both the man and the horse were similar was an odd coincidence. However, the fact that they both had fossil-like qualities was not too unusual for this area. A number of major fossil deposits have been discovered in western South Dakota ranging from ammonites to dinosaurs. Kate remembered as a child finding Baculites embedded in the cliffs along the river. They were still a part of her collection. She would send this piece to her office for identification, and hopefully, the results of the first specimen would match this one.

Chapter Five

Dinner in Dupree

Almost every small town in the Dakotas has a supper club, the establishment where people go to socialize, have a better-than-average local meal, and party on the weekends. Dupree was no exception although the City Club was a bit smaller and less fancy than most. Generally it was the townspeople who frequented the club, occasionally local ranchers and farmers came in for a night on the town, and always the young adults came to the bar for weekend entertainment which often included a country/western band and dancing. Conspicuously not present at the Club were the local Indians. The unspoken word made it as off limits for Indians, and while no one prohibited them from entering the establishment, it was with some certainty that a fight would likely ensue between the locals and the Indian unfortunate enough to have violated the rule. It had always been that way, and the nineties hadn't brought about the broader acceptance of cultural differences present in other parts of the country. John Redbull would probably be accepted at the City Club. He was educated and a leader in the community, and if he did have dinner there he would likely be in the company of whites or other tribal leaders. Kathryn new these rules and recognized that if John had accompanied her this evening, while there would have been no trouble, the environment may have been uncomfortable for him. Like moving in and out of a time warp, Kate pondered the philosophical differences in American culture. In Miami differences arose not only between races, but between cultures among races. Puerto Ricans, South Americans, and Cubans were all Hispanic, yet their cultures could be worlds apart. Jamaicans, Haitians, and African Americans could all be Black, yet feelings of superiority and inferiority was prevalent among those groups as well; Jamaicans looking down upon African Americans for lack of ambition, and Haitians, the most recent of South Florida's refugees, falling at the bottom of the cultural ladder. We are all tribal by nature, she thought, somehow reverting to a primitive state where food gathering has been replaced by the gathering of economic wealth and spears have evolved to automatic weapons. Why should South Dakota be different? Enmeshed in this isolated beauty is a history of cultural dominance for economic gain; U.S. government vs. local Indian tribes, cattle companies vs. Indian tribes, ranchers vs. homesteaders, and gold mining industrialists vs. Indians, ranchers, and the government. The Homestake Mine, largest and longest running gold mining operation in the continental United States was founded by the Hearst family. The wealth from the mine, while providing economic stability to the region for over a century, nonetheless, was ultimately funneled to the coffers of the wealthy. So yes, this sparsely populated, unspoiled land of western South Dakota was simply a microcosm of civilized culture. Having reflected on these sociological facts, Kathryn, hair tied back and dressed in a dark wool skirt, brushed silk blouse, and brown suede jacket turned the ignition on her Jeep and headed toward the City Club.

Sam Pickens was engaged in conversation at the bar when she arrived. Looking up with an acknowledgment of her presence he motioned to the waitress to show her to a table and returned to the conversation. He was talking with two men, one dressed in khaki with a gray beard and neatly groomed salt and pepper hair, the other, much younger, and in jeans and western shirt. The gray-haired man, with the appearance of a professor or scientist, didn't look like a local. Pickens finally reached for his drink, excused himself from the group and walked toward the table. The other two men paid the bartender and left.

Sam slid into the booth across from Kathryn. "Sorry for keeping you waiting," he drawled. "Had some business to take care of. You sure do look pretty. Is that suede?"

"Thank you, Sam, yes, it's one of my favorite jackets."

"So where ya'll from Ms. Kathryn. I saw that card said Florida. Must be pretty important work you doin' to bring you all the way up here"

"Well, as I'm sure you also saw on my card I'm a forensics investigator, and was asked by some of my colleagues to assist them in an investigation." Her judgment told her not to share with him that she grew up here, nor that she was helping an old friend. The less he knew about her, the better. "I'm curious, from your accent it sounds like you're not a Dakota native."

"Nope, we moved here from Oklahoma a few years ago. Bought 1,500 acres to raise some cattle and Appaloosa horses. We breed about the finest Appaloosas in the country. You familiar with the breed?" Winters are pretty bad up here but land's cheap and there's lots of it. That is, if the Indians don't take it all back. They're trying to. Hope you don't take offense, working for them and all."

"Actually," she replied, "I'm trying to stay out of local politics since I don't know enough about the situation to have an opinion." Kathryn ordered T-bone steak, baked potato and a salad, remembering that even though salmon and lobster tail were on the menu, it had traveled more than a thousand miles in a frozen state to reach this establishment and most likely didn't resemble the seafood she was used to.

"So Sam, tell me about how the horse ended up on your ranch. When did it appear?" she asked.

"Oh, it must have been about the 15th of November when my ranch hands were loading horses and found him near the fence of the south pasture. They took him back to the ranch. We thought it was strange that he was saddled and all, so we made some phone calls and checked in town to see if anybody was missing a horse. Thought he probably bucked off the rider and ran. I heard some time later that the sheepherder was missing and thought maybe it was his horse, but nobody came to claim him so I just put him out to pasture. Ya know, maybe that horse did buck him off and he died out there? Too bad, wish we had gone looking for him but there's a lot of land out there and chances are we wouldn't have found him anyway. Say, where did they find him?"

"Sorry Sam, I'm not a liberty to say right now. It will probably come out in the local paper when the police report is released, but until then I really can't share much information. You say he came in from the south. That would mean he came through reservation land, right?"

"Yup, and that pastureland backs up to Rassmusson's place." He paused, then added, "It's pretty rugged country out there. Not very accessible except by horseback. Don't you think about going out there. It's just badlands and rattlesnakes."

"Yes," she added, "So I've heard." Kate knew that there were no major badlands in that area and certainly it was far too cold for the rattlers to come out of their dens. So Pickens didn't want her searching that area. Why? Her next query was posed simply to get a reaction. "In fact, I've been told that where the soil washes away in the badlands, they've found a number of fossil deposits. Have you come across any fossils out there?"

Sam Pickens eyes darted up to hers. "Well...well, I don't know." Regaining composure, he added, "I've never gone out looking for them, but I understand that people have come upon some fossils up in the hills. Nothing significant around here though."

Once again Kathryn detected that the rancher was making an effort to cover up something. Why would he tell her that no significant fossil discoveries were made in the area, when the largest and most complete specimen of Tyrannosaurus Rex had been found only a few miles east of this area? She had, herself, found specimens in the very area he described. If, in fact, the sheepherder had been killed in an area of fossil deposits, did Sam Pickens know something about the murder?

Sam Pickens motioned for the waitress and looking at Kathryn asked, "How 'bout an after dinner drink? Maybe we could move over to the bar and relax for a while."

"No thanks, Sam" she replied. "I have some work to do tonight and really have to be going." She handed a credit card to the waitress, but Sam reached for the tab.

"No, no, you let me get this pretty lady. And maybe we can go out again while you're here. You must be getting pretty lonesome here by yourself, working with nothing but the Indians. I'd like to show you around a little. It'd be my pleasure," he said looking suggestively into her eyes.

"I'm sure you would, Sam, but somehow I get the feeling that your wife might not approve. She added, attempting to remain composed, "And I'm far too busy to be lonely. Don't you worry about me, I'm being well cared for by John Redbull and his family. They're excellent hosts."

Kathryn breathed deeply as she walked out into the crisp cold air. She looked up at a black sky and saw nothing but thousands of twinkling stars. Relieved to have finished her meeting with Sam Pickens, she was anxious to get back to the cottage, snuggle into her sweats and begin to review the faxes that had arrived from U of M.

Her phone was ringing as she opened the cottage door. It was John at the end of the line. "Kate, I'm glad you're home. I want to know about your meeting, but first I wanted you to know that we are releasing information about the murder tomorrow morning, so be prepared for inquiries about your role in all of this. Also, I hope your ready for a hard ride tomorrow. Thought we'd get the horses and ride up to the sight in the morning."

"I'll have my boots on," she quipped. "And I'll fill you in on the meeting tomorrow. Oh, by the way, are the photos developed yet?"

"Almost forgot, yes, they are finished and I'll have JR run them by tonight. Just a lot of prairie scenes. Don't know if they can help you any."

Tearing yards of paper from the Fax, she began browsing test results; blood type O+, finger prints confirmed as victim's, prints match on film canister, rock fragments evaluated and assessed to be fossil material from freshwater shale and sandstone deposits probably from the Late Cretaceous period and consistent with the structure and composition of dinosaur fossil remains of that period. She suspected that the sample found in the horse's hoof would show comparable features.

Kate switched on the desk lamp and pulled photos out of the envelope that JR had delivered. She closely inspected each of the pictures; sheep grazing near a creek, a lone White-tail buck standing guard on crest of a hill, a purple western sunset behind a range of prairie hills, a shot of a camper trailer nestled against the cutbank of the same hills, a sloping view from the top of a hill looking down upon a ravine, another photo of the ravine at a closer vantage point showing a tiny focal point of activity about two-thirds of the way down. Only seven photos had been taken, the remainder of the 24-print roll was not exposed. "So," Kathryn pondered, "Wesley Johnson started shooting a roll of film, then removed it from the camera and left it in his jeans pocket. Why?" It was certain that the pictures would be helpful in finding the exact location of his camp. She could also use them to identify the area surrounding him. But she was most interested in the pictures of the ravine and spec of activity on the slope. Using a magnifying ring she attempted to get a better view of the activity, but an enlarged print would be needed if she were to identify the action. The photo should be computerized, then digitally enhanced. Tomorrow, however, she had enough information to search the area. As she mulled over the photographs, her thoughts were suddenly interrupted by the sound of a vehicle passing in front of the window. She glanced up to see the dark outline of a pickup truck driving slowly down her street with its lights out. Bars are closed she thought, and that's an accident waiting to happen.

Chapter Six

Riding a Horse Named Shania Twain

Kathryn awoke early the next morning in preparation for the long day ahead. She dressed in jeans, boots, and a warm flannel shirt. Exhilarated and yet somewhat apprehensive about the ride, she began packing her gear. Kate had learned to ride at age three and by the time she was a teenager was competing in rodeos as a barrel racer. It was the only event open to women at the time. She was a good horsewoman but hadn't been near a horse in over ten years. Knowing that John would expect to see the agility of the teenager he had remembered, her ego wasn't prepared to let him see any less. So while the ride should go well, her legs probably would refuse to move the next morning!

In her leather bag, Kate packed sandwiches, water, a thermos of hot coffee, bananas and an apple. She also brought binoculars, a flash light, specimen bottles and plastic bags, her Canon 35mm with 300 zoom lens, a digital camera, and a 32 caliber Baretta.

As she pulled her Jeep into John Redbull's yard, she saw a man and woman leading horses to the loading shoot. A large trailer was backed to the coral, and as she stepped from the truck she could here the horses stomping up the shute and into the trailer. "Morning Kate," John shouted as swung the gate up and into place. "I'd like you to meet Sue Badger. I asked her to ride with us today."

Kathryn approached the woman in the corral. She was dressed in the green uniform of a park ranger, stood about 5'11", with incredibly long, straight black hair and piercing dark eyes. "Kate, I finally get to meet you," she said with a smile, holding her hand through the corral fence to shake Kathryn's.

"Sue is with the Department of Forestry. She's responsible for land management in this area and knows the territory real well. I thought she would a big help in locating our sites."

Sue Badger had worked for the Bureau of Land Management for nine years. Holding what was typically thought of as a "man's" job, she had worked her way from mending government pasture fences to head of Land Management for the region. As such, she was responsible for grassland preservation and control, coordinating cattle movement within the pastures, fire control, and enforcement of unauthorized use of the property. She had been the initial contact when the boys discovered Wes Johnson, and she had assisted in recovering the body. In her early 30s and in excellent physical condition, Sue had a formidable presence. Her height and broad shoulders left no doubt that she could hold her own in most situations. When she spoke, however, the gentle tone of her voice comforted the unwary. Kate sensed that she would like Sue and that she would be a helpful addition to the team.

Their next stop with the pickup and trailer was Tom Crowfeather's ranch. As the pickup bounced through mud ruts in the trail leading to his house, Kathryn was amazed to see that almost nothing had changed from the time she visited the ranch with her father. A junk yard of old cars and farm implements lined the fence along the road. Several horses grazed among a flock of chickens and five or six mixed-mutt dogs, and wood smoke curled from the chimney. The only apparent additions were the electric lines running from the main road to the yard and a small satellite dish mounted on the side of the house. Even Tom Crowfeather was exposed to the 21st Century.

Tom's Tennessee walking horse was beautiful. The buckskin mare, named Shania, was slender, but stout, and had a gentle disposition. The horse nuzzled her arm as Kate led her to the trailer. Kate breathed a sigh of relief as her fears of riding a wild bronc were calmed.

"The horse's name is Shania, after that girl singer." Tom Crowfeather proclaimed. "I like her. She's on my TV, and she's just like a wild horse. They say her father was Indian."

Kathryn laughed at the thought of riding a horse named Shania Twain, and at the idea that old Tom Crowfeather watched videos via satellite TV. For an old man who had spent most of his life without indoor plumbing or electricity, who had witnessed the advent of automobiles and airplanes, telephone, radio and now satellite television, Tom was living testament to his generation's adaptability to change. She loved him for this.

After taking a few moments to meet Crowfeather's son and grandson, they left the ranch, heading south on Highway 73 towards the Cheyenne River. Several miles south of Faith, the Cheyenne River winds through uninhabited pastureland. Sue, Kate, and John packed the saddle bags, saddled the horses and began the journey to the hills directly east of the road. They followed the riverbed for about an hour, nearing the range of buttes. Kathryn found herself returning to her old habit of scanning the ground beneath her, searching for arrowheads. But today she saw nothing more than a decomposed shotgun shell casing and an aluminum can. The three riders talked about their respective jobs, their families, and their attachment to the land. Sue stopped as they neared the hills and indicated that it was time to turn south and begin to ascend the hillside. They let their horses drink at the river while Kate poured hot coffee for the riders. They then continued south to the sloping hills. About a third of the way up the hill, Sue stopped again, and shifting back in the saddle turned to John and Kate. "Over there," she pointed to the left, "is the cave entrance." After another five minutes' ride, they dismounted and approached an opening in the hillside. Comprised of shale and sand, the cave entrance measured about 10 feet across and 5 feet high. The walls quickly narrowed forming a small dark tunnel. Already, Kathryn's eyes were scanning the site, looking for signs of activity.

"We found the body here," Susan said, pointing to right side of the entrance. Kathryn could make out footprints in the sand below, but the dirt was too soft to leave recognizable imprints. "Besides," she thought, "Too many people had been at the site for prints to be meaningful."

"John, I'd like you and Sue to search the area in and around here for anything — cigarette butts, wrappers, fibers, anything." She then scooped up a patch of earth that appeared to have been soaked with dark substance and placed it in a specimen bottle. Suddenly John yelled, "Hey, come over here when you're done. I think I've found something." Almost buried in the sand at the foot of the narrowing tunnel was a silver colored metal instrument. Kate leaned over and taking a bandanna from her pocket, used it to pick up the item.

"Damn," said John, "it looks like some kind of knife."

Kathryn looked at it. It was a scalpel but it didn't look like any surgical instrument she was familiar with. "Hey, Sue, have you ever seen anything that looks like this?" asked Kate.

"Yeh, last time I threatened my doctor! No, seriously, it looks like the kind of tool the rock hunters use to clean up their specimens. I watched them preparing fossils down at the School of Mines one time, and that's the kind of tools they had."

At that moment, a few more pieces of the puzzle began to fall in to place, as she considered the slash wound to the abdomen that was detailed in the pathology report. The tool might have been used to make that slashing wound to the abdomen. And, since according to the autopsy, the wound had been inflicted after death, it likely had occurred here in the cave. The death blow to the head, however, had not occurred here. There was nothing to show that the victim was alive in the cave. He had most likely been killed elsewhere and brought to the cave. But there was still no logical explanation for the stabbing. With the discovery of the tool, however, they had an important piece of information. While it wasn't the murder weapon, it was an important key to the investigation, a key that seemed to be leading to a connection with paleontology. Kate turned to her associates and sternly proclaimed, "I don't want anyone to know about this find, or for that matter, that we have even been here! Our investigation is leading us in a direction that might become complicated and even dangerous, and I don't think it's wise for anyone to know what we've discovered or what we're doing."

"Well, I'm not one to be afraid of anything," replied Sue.

"Nobody messes with me around here, and if you're with me, nobody will mess with you either."

John interrupted, "Sue, I hear what you're saying but I think Kate believes that this might be more than just a small town murder. There could be a lot of people in on this, and they might not be from around here, right Kate?"

"Well, I'm not saying that exactly, but there are a lot of signs pointing to Wesley Johnson's involvement in something bigger than sheep herding, something having to do with fossils. That's about all I know now."

John stood up and motioned to the women. "I wanted to ride further into the hills where Johnson's trailer was found but its already 3:00 so I guess we better head home. Tomorrow we'll ride up to those hills."

As Kathryn moved toward the horses, she could feel her legs weaken. They were bowed and cramped, and the thought of riding again tomorrow made her wince. "Hey girl, you doin' OK?" John asked as he grabbed her around the waste.

"Of course I am," she stubbornly replied. Never would she admit to him or to the other woman that she, Kate Stafford, was cold and stiff and that her bones ached to the marrow from one day on a horse. I may be a soft city girl she thought as she mounted the buckskin, but my pride will never let it show!

The ride back to the highway somehow seemed shorter, as the riders discussed their findings and hypotheses as to what had occurred in these hills.

Had the sheep herder been involved in a site excavation? Who had he been working with?

Or was he simply a bystander who had come upon information that someone wished to keep secret. Was the wound inflicted after his death meant to serve as a message? Was it ritualistic, or was it meant lead the investigation in another direction? Perhaps the killers wanted it to look like a savage attack; something a crazed Indian might do? All were somewhat plausible explanations, but Kathryn knew that the truth could only be found by methodically examining the evidence they had and assembling it in a logical sequence. There were still many missing pieces. By the time they arrived back at the truck and trailer, the subject had changed to a hot meal, and the drive home was marked by weary silence. They agreed to meet early the next morning to continue the search. Kate gratefully steered her Jeep toward home, knowing that there was still work to be done, but too tired and sore to continue.

Kathryn could barely move her legs out of the Jeep when she arrived home. Removing a bottle of Absorbine Junior from her overnight bag, she collapsed on the sofa and pulled the boots from her weary feet. As she switched on the TV and nestled back into the sofa, an eerie feeling came over her. Something didn't feel right. There was a faint odor of cologne in the room. Jumping to her feet, Kate walked to the desk. She was certain that her files were not in the order in which she had left them this morning. File folders were out of order and papers were haphazardly placed in the files. "Damn," she thought. "I should have known better. Being in the middle of nowhere is no excuse for relaxing security. These papers would never have been left on a desk top in my office at home."

She immediately dialed John's number. "Sorry to interrupt your supper but I need to know if any of your people may have been in my cottage today." John indicated that no one had permission to be in her house and had no reason to be there. "I'm very concerned, John," she replied. "Somebody definitely was here, and they were looking for something. They went through my files."

John was disturbed. "Look, I'll have a locking file cabinet sent over in the morning. We're also going to have the lock changed on your door. Do you want JR to come over and spend the night?"

"No, I'm sure I'll be all right. I have a weapon and I'll make sure the doors and windows are secured. You know, late last night I saw a car with its lights out cruise by the house. Didn't think anything of it at the time. If you have any pull with the local police department, you might casually ask them to patrol the house, but I don't want them investigating the break in. I'd rather we do that ourselves."

"Sure thing, Kate. I'll make sure someone keeps an eye on your place. If anything at all seems suspicious, you call me, understand?" She could sense that he was concerned and would probably station himself outside her door.

As she secured the house Kathryn analyzed the situation. Someone wanted to know what she was doing and perhaps how much information she had accumulated. But who knew where she was staying? They easily could have followed her home, and it was likely that the town gossips knew where she lived, if not what she was doing here. Fortunately, not much information had been accumulated in the folders — the autopsy report and the test results from Miami. The test results, however, did made reference to the fossil fragments, and the autopsy confirmed the secondary wound had been made after death, both pieces of information that she preferred to have kept confidential. If the killer knew she had these facts, then they also knew the direction that the investigation was taking.

Kate jumped as the phone rang. It was George Nealy from her lab in Miami. "Kathryn, I have the photo enhancements for you and I want to download them onto your laptop. I think you'll find some interesting results. Looks like several people loading a trailer. Hope that means something to you."

"It sure does, George. Thanks for your usual good job. I'll talk to you tomorrow about some other evidence I'm looking at. Please assign a job and billing number to this project. We're likely to see a lot more evidence than I had expected run through the lab. Also, George, we need to be certain that we run all computer and fax files through a secure line. I've got some security issues up here."

Having completed her instructions to Nealy, the modem connection was established, and Kathryn watched as the files materialized on the screen. When she had finished downloading the files she transferred the six picture files one by one to the printer. What emerged surprised her but helped to confirm her suspicions. Each photo showed in varying degrees of clarity and close-up, three men loading materials into a trailer. She couldn't identify the faces of the men from the photos, but the trailer was definitely a horse trailer, one that looked a lot like the trailer Sam Pickens was loading when they visited his ranch. Sam Pickens had said that they were loading Appaloosa horses the day that

Johnson's saddle horse appeared. But horses weren't present in any of these photos and whatever was being loaded into the trailer certainly was not the size of a horse. Tomorrow she would search for the location where the photographs had been taken.

Chapter Seven

Get Out of Town

Though Kate was exhausted, she didn't sleep well that night, partly because of the pain in her legs, but mostly because of the break-in and the photos of the trailer. The bed smelled like the Absorbine Junior that lie soaking into her thigh muscles, and the wind outside was thrashing a tree branch against the bedroom window. Her insomnia surely heightened all of these senses.

By daybreak, she was up and packed for the day. She had repacked most of the same gear, adding only the photos, a foldable shovel and a tape measure. Swinging the leather bag over her shoulder, she headed to the car. But she stopped short when she noticed a letter left at the door of her cottage. The white letter-sized envelope had been placed inside the storm door. Thinking it probably a note for her left by John or JR, she hastily tore it open. On a white sheet of paper a warning had been typed:

Lady

> *I f you want to stay healthy, stop putting your nose where it doesn't belong. I suggest you leave town now, and forget about helping these Indians. It's none of your affair and any more snooping will cost you and your friends more than you are willing to pay. Just wrap up your investigation*

> *nice and easy. Tell them you don't have enough evidence to*
> *make any kind of case and get out of here.*

Kathryn was both angry and frightened. As a forensics investigator, she wasn't accustomed to criminal threats. Law enforcement officers were sometimes threatened, but as scientists, forensics personnel were usually too far removed from the crime to be targets. This was different. Just now, she knew more than anyone else about the crime, and someone didn't want her knowledge used.

Turning back to enter the house, Kathryn locked the door behind her and picked up the telephone. "John," she said urgently, "I know its early, but I need you over here now!"

"I'm on my way," was the reply.

John Redbull carefully examined the letter. "What do we do now?" he asked. "Kate, I'm more concerned about your safety than solving this crime. If you want to pack up and go home, I understand. You've been a big help already, and we can take it from here."

"Hell no," she shouted. "I'm not about to be intimidated by a letter. All it means is that we're getting close to the truth and its making somebody pretty nervous."

"Then its time to get the Tribal Police involved. We need to have some protection over here!" said John.

Kathryn agreed. "I think its time to turn all our evidence over to them," she said. "It's also time to issue some search warrants. I want someone to get out to Sam Picken's place and confiscate the horse and tack. I also want a warrant to pick up Wesley Johnson's trailer and its contents. This all needs to happen today before its too late, if it isn't already." She was clearly disgusted with herself for handling this case too loosely. In an effort to be low key about the investigation, she had jeprodized the case and their safety.

John placed a call to Tribal Headquarters in Eagle Butte.

He asked that the Tribal authorities meet them in Dupree that morning. Relieved that he had already turned the case over to them days earlier, he was confident that they would be able to cooperate and effectively coordinate their work. Nonetheless, it would be important for he and Kathryn to complete the job that they had begun. He hoped to meet with the officers this morning, leaving the afternoon free to continue their search of the hills. He placed a call to Sue Badger, asking her to pick up the horses and to wait for them near the Rassmussen ranch. It was then decided that the police would secure Kathryn's files and move them to John's office where they would be safe. As for Kathryn, he preferred that she relocate to his home. If not, he would make certain that the cottage was well guarded while she was home.

By 9:30 that morning that Tribal Police had arrived at Kathryn's cottage. The note was turned over to the officers and while one man searched the area surrounding the house, the lead officer met with John and Kathryn. Mark Uses- Knives had been with the Tribal Police since he was 25. Now in his early 40s, he was a seasoned officer and had handled most of the important cases prosecuted on the Cheyenne Reservation. While most cases involved domestic violence, drunk and disorderly, property disputes, and theft, there were occasionally cases involving major felonies including murder. Uses-Knives investigated them.

With typical Native American cautiousness, Mark Uses-Knives approached Kathryn in a respectful, yet distrusting manner. "So, Ms. Stafford, er... I should say Dr. Stafford, I understand you have been working with John Redbull on the Johnson murder. Are you here in an official capacity from Florida?"

"I was asked by Mr. Redbull to assist him in pulling together evidence for the case. John and I have known each other since childhood. I grew up in this area and our families have been friends for years. He was aware of my forensics background, so we both thought I could be of assistance in pulling together some preliminary information and lab tests. Now that we've pretty much completed our work, I'd like to turn our findings over to you."

"So you're here kind of unofficially?" he asked again, not yet comfortable with her explanation.

"Yes, I guess you could say it is unofficial," she replied. Deciding that a dose of the truth was the best cure for his apprehension, she added, "I have a fair amount of competence as a forensic investigator, and I'm pretty well known in the profession, mostly from my books and articles related to the subject. When John and I spoke about this case, he was concerned that the Feds would come in and that tensions would escalate between the tribe and the community. I hope you will agree with us that its better for everyone if this case is solved quietly with local law enforcement."

"Well, I can't disagree with that reasoning. I've always tried to keep our local problems here on the reservation under the control of the Tribal Counsel. We've all seen just how crazy it gets when the Feds get involved. Seems like everybody suffers. The Feds walk away, and we still have the same problems we've always had, sometimes more."

"I know," replied Stafford, "And I'm here to help you avoid that in any way that I can."

"I respect John's decisions," Uses-Knives pronounced. "He has done a lot of good work for the tribe. If he trusts you in these matters, then I guess I trust you too."

"I thank you for that trust," she answered. "And I'd like to fill you in on what we have found so far when you have the time."

Kate and John spent the next two hours briefing the police officer on their findings. Kathryn gave him copies of her forensic lab reports, but held back the photo enhancements. She wanted to investigate the site herself, before alerting the authorities or the criminals to the progress of her search.

John seemed pleased with the results of their meeting. It had never been his intent to exclude the local authorities from the investigation. It was, after all, their job and not his. But by providing some top notch data, he hoped their job could be made easier, thereby eliminating the need for outside help. They seemed to be meeting that objective.

Chapter Eight

The Fossil Patch

Just after noon, John and Kathryn met Susan Badger at the entrance to the Rassmussen ranch. "Boy, am I glad to see you," Sue exclaimed. "I was beginnin' to think I'd be out here all day. What the hell is going on in town? Your wife said you left for Kate's at dawn and that the Tribal Police were on their way to see you."

Kate and John explained the events of the previous night and morning while they saddled the horses and loaded their packs.

"Well, Shania Twain," said Kate to the little buckskin mare. "You look pretty chipper today. Look what I have for you," she whispered as she took an apple from her pocket. The horse whinnied softly and took the apple in her teeth.

Sue motioned to a ravine just ahead, "The quickest ride to the campsite is up that ravine and across those hills. Can't be more than three or four miles." With that, they mounted the horses and set a brisk pace up the ravine.

As they crossed the first group of hills, another ridge appeared in the distance. Kate pulled out the photos and looked for comparable setting. "Over there, this picture resembles those hills."

"Yup," Sue acknowledged, "That would be just about where he set up camp." They turned the horses in the direction of the ridge, and after riding for another 45 minutes approached the sight of the cutbank where Wes Johnson's trailer had been parked. A thorough search of the campsite revealed no more than the remnants of the sheepherder's garbage, too decomposed to search or identify.

"I want to ride up there," Sue pointed to the hill above. "I believe that may be where he shot those last photos."

As they reached the crest of the hill, Kathryn again pulled the photos from her pocket and scanned the slope below. "That's it," she shouted. "That's the spot on the picture!"

They quickly descended. About two-thirds of the way down the hill, Kate found what she had been searching for. It was the sight where the horse trailer had been parked. She jumped off the horse and cautiously stepped toward a series of mounds. The site appeared to be excavated in an area of about 60 x 100 feet. The holes and trenches varied in depth from one to four feet. At the end of the dig site were a series of tire tracks and footprints. The trio spread out over the area, searching for clues. Kathryn wanted to find evidence that Wes Johnson had been on the site. A slim chance, she knew, but it might identify the sight of the murder. If Johnson was a part of the excavation party, why would they kill him? On the other hand, if he came upon this activity by accident, what were the men taking from the area that lead them to murder a witness? She felt certain this sight held the answers to those questions.

"Hey, Kathryn, over here. A cigarette pack. You want it?"

"Of course," she replied. "Even if its a cigarette butt, I want it." She, on the other hand was looking for other evidence, the potential murder weapon — a fossilized bone. Using a piece of screen she had found at the cottage, she sifted through soil in several of the holes, searching for fossil fragments that might match those she had already analyzed.

Sue called out again, "I found something else, looks like a rubber thing. Come and take a look at it."

Sue had found a black rubber stub, the kind of thing that was placed on chair legs to prevent slipping and movement. Kate looked at it carefully. A light bulb switched on! This was the rubber end of a crutch or cane, maybe the walking cane that had been inventoried in Johnson's personal belongings at the autopsy. They may have just found a piece of evidence that would link Wesley Johnson to this site, the sight of the murder. They began to cautiously search the immediate area, looking for signs of a struggle. Too many months had passed, however, for blood or tissue evidence to remain in tact. But Kathryn finally found the piece of fossilized material she had been seeking, and these two pieces, the cane stub and the fossil remains, could prove to be vital in solving the case.

Kathryn knew that the site couldn't be thoroughly searched in one afternoon. She had neither the tools nor the time to do an adequate investigation, so she would ask Mark Uses-Knives to send in a team to the finish the job. For now, they had enough evidence to proceed to the next level of the investigation. Having connected Wesley Johnson with the excavation site, they now could focus on the purpose of the dig and identity of the men loading the trailer.

Pleased with the day's findings, they loaded the horses and drove east toward Dupree just as the sun was setting. They discussed plans for tomorrow, and John shared his concerns about Kathryn's safety. For that matter, he was now concerned about the safety of all three of them. Susan lived by herself just outside of town in a small farm house supplied by the Bureau of Land Management. And while John lived in town with his family, as he saw it, they were all vulnerable. Whoever had sent the note was probably watching their movements, and if one person had been killed to cover up their activities there was no reason to believe that it couldn't happen again.

John could even sense fear in Susan's eyes as he explained his concerns. He couldn't remember having observed Susan Badger fearful of anything. She had wrangled angry bulls, broken up fights between drunken, burley men, and worked through blizzard white-out conditions. Yet tonight she appeared nervous.

As the pickup turned into Rudbull's drive, Sue broke her silence. "Kate," she said pensively, "I've got an idea, if its OK with you and John. How about if I stayed at your cottage for a while? I could bring my dogs. They're good protection, and we both might feel safer."

Kathryn looked questioningly at John. He responded positively to the suggestion. "If you're comfortable with it Kate, I think its a good idea for both of you. There's safety in numbers and although the police are patrolling your house, the dogs give good protection too."

So it was settled. Sue would pick up her dogs and move into town until things calmed down. Kathryn was comfortable with the arrangement even though she was protective of her privacy. Sue didn't seem overly talkative or the type to pry. She would probably be good company, and Kate would feel more secure knowing someone else was in the house.

Later that evening, Sue moved a few things into Kathryn's cottage: the two dogs, a German Shepherd and a Husky, one large bag of dog food, and over-and-under double barrel shot gun, a bag of groceries, and a twelve-pack of Hamms beer. "This was definitely a prairie woman," Kate thought. "Kind of like having Calamity Jane move in! Yes, this was certainly going to be an interesting experience."

Sue Badger had a reputation as an eccentric with a heart of gold. She had never married, never dated that anyone remembered. Her family had lived on a small farm on Cherry Creek, south of Dupree. Her father was White, her mother Indian, making her in local terms, a half-breed. Those who knew the family remember her father as a cruel man who barely provided for his wife and children. Until she died at age 35, Susan's mother provided for the family, tending a garden and raising goats and chickens to feed herself and three children. Sue, the oldest child, took on adult responsibilities at an early age. Her father was rarely home and when he was, he was an unwelcome visitor. Harold Badger was a horse trader, but in truth spent most of his time at the local bars planning "get-rich" schemes and terrorizing the locals. The kindest act he bestowed upon Susan, between the beatings and abuse, was the gift of a horse. She spent hours, sometimes days, riding in the hills, hunting for deer and antelope. Some people said she could communicate with the animals. Her special sensitivity to them, a gift often found in children who are physically abused, enabled her to develop a unique closeness and trust with wildlife.

When Sue's mother died, the children were moved to Eagle Butte where they attended government school. Given the opportunity to live more securely with her siblings, she flourished in her studies, graduating from high school with honors. She attended a two-year college in Rapid City, but returned to the reservation upon graduation and took a job with the Forestry Service. Since then, she had worked hard and enjoyed an active, albeit reclusive life with her animals. Sue could always be counted on to provide help when needed, and was often called upon to treat the neighbors' ailing livestock and pets. Well loved by the local children, she also always found time to help them with 4-H and rodeo projects. No one seemed to know very much about her dreams or aspirations, only that she appeared to live peacefully, well balanced with nature and those around her.

Chapter Nine

The Dinosaurs

With a second verification that the stone fragments she had submitted to her lab for identification were dinosaur bones, Kathryn determined that she needed to learn more about dinosaurs and the prevalence of fossil deposits in the area. After briefing the investigating team who would comb the area in and around the dig site, she departed in the direction of Rapid City and the South Dakota School of Mines and Technology.

The "Dakota School of Mines" was established in 1880. At the time, the school's primary mission was to provide a supply of engineers and mining technicians for nearby mining operations in the Black Hills. In particular, The Homestake Mining Company had taken an interest in the local college.

The Homestake Lead had been discovered in 1876 by two brothers, Moses and Fred Manuel. The brothers soon sold the rich lead vein of gold to George Hearst. Hearst, the father of William Randolf Hearst, was a miner. Whether through luck or a prospector's intuitive sense of geology, George Hearst ended up owning interest in some of the most important mining operations in the United States — the Comstock Load, the Anaconda Copper Mines in Montana, and the Homestake Mine in South Dakota. As a child, the Indians had referred to him as "boy that the earth talks to". As a man, the earth offered him fortunes that were to build an empire.

The South Dakota School of Mines & Technology received funding from Hearst and the Homestake Mining Company for many years so as to assure that engineers were trained in the latest technologies. Now the Homestake Mining operations have dwindled to a skeleton crew, and the Mining Company's donations fund the geology department of the more prominent U.C., Berkley. But SDSM&T continues to have an established reputation in the field of engineering. It is also well known for its Department of Geology and its graduate program in Paleontology. SDSM&T is one of the few universities to afford its degree candidates the opportunity to conduct field research locally in some of the most fossil-rich areas in the country.

Kathryn smiled as she walked up the steps of the building housing the college's Museum of Geology. She'd been in this museum many times before, always marveling at the huge dinosaurs and case after case of mineral specimens. She wondered what she would be doing today had she accepted the School of Mines invitation to study here. She had opted instead to attend med school at Georgetown University. She had been anxious to leave the state then, and engineering wasn't the area she had wanted to pursue. Besides, at that time she would have been the only female student at SDSM&T, a situation that as a teenager she had found somewhat intimidating.

Kathryn introduced herself to the staff in the Department of Geology, secured geological maps from the museum book store, and proceeded to the paleontology section of the university library. She wanted to identify Western South Dakota's geological strata and then correlate those prehistoric periods with the terrestrial species of the time.

Cross referencing the geological maps with a key to fossil- bearing rock strata in the region, she noted that the area around and north of the Cheyenne River was primarily made up of shale deposits from the Upper Cretaceous and Upper Cretaceous Marine period. The Cretaceous period occurred in the later half and close of the Mesozoic Era, marking the second largest mass extinction ever recorded. Almost half of all animal species were destroyed, including all of the dinosaurs, all of the ammonoids, and two-thirds of all corals. Mammals were the only category of animals to seemingly escape the massacre. The cause of this mass extinction is unknown, although a most popular theory speculates that the earth was hit by a large meteorite about 65 million years ago, bringing an end to the Mesozoic Era. The surface strata of the central western part of South Dakota bore the remnants of that mass extinction. Other areas of Western North America also harbored the same strata, principally eastern Colorado, the southwestern tip of Wyoming, north central Montana, and southern Saskatchewan.

The fossilization process that took place at the time of cataclysm left us with an X-ray, of sorts, of the animal life that inhabited the planet over 65 million years ago. That process began at the time of death. The soft parts of the animal begin to decompose quickly due to the environment and ultimately the tissue is totally destroyed. Those remaining parts containing a high mineral content, including bones and teeth, remain in tact longer and over time undergo a chemical process leading to fossilization. The most common method of fossil formation is called mineralization — a process where the original organic substance is completely replaced by a mineral. These minerals include calcium carbonate in the form of calcite, quartz, opal, or chalcedony. Less frequently the fossil is made up of pyrite, limonite or gypsum.

During the Upper Cretaceous period, tribes of dinosaurs roamed the plains, some carnivorous, others herbivorous. Among the largest and most ferocious was the Tyrannosaurus. Weighing about 10 tons and reaching a height of 20 feet, the Tyrannosaurus terrorized the earth about 75 million years ago, and fed on other herbivorous dinosaurs. The Psittacosaurus also roamed the earth during the Upper Cretaceous period. It was a small animal, 3-to-4 feet in length with a head resembling a parrot's skull with beak. Also known to exist in the period was the Triceratops, a large (20-30 feet in length) four-footed dinosaur with a skull resembling the rhinosaurus.

Ferocious in appearance, this animal's armor served as protection, since the creature was an herbivour. She read on, documenting the list of prehistoric life that was known to have inhabited this land millions of years ago.

Kathryn also noted that South Dakota was one of the premier sites in North America for dinosaur and marine fossil remains of this period. This area and central Montana had recently been the sight of several major paleontology finds. Piecing this information together with the site she was investigating, she was sure that there was an important connection.

Having recorded the information she needed, Kathryn packed her notes and began stacking the research materials on the corner of the library table. She glanced up to see an interestingly looking man staring at her. He was dressed in khaki pants, hiking boots, and a plaid shirt. His hair was a neatly trimmed salt-and-pepper gray, and his eyes twinkled. He got up from the chair and walked toward her.

"I hope you're not offended by my stare," he offered, "but I couldn't help noticing that for hours you have been intensely absorbed in the paleontology section. Are you a student here?"

"No," replied Kathryn, "just doing some research on the subject. Are you an instructor here at the college?"

"Not exactly," he said. "I'm a guest lecturer in paleontology studies. I'm sorry, my name is Dr. Fromm, and you are?" He extended his hand.

"Well, Dr. Fromm," she responded, not accustomed to exchanging titles as well as names outside of business, "I'm Dr. Stafford."

"Hmm, MD or PhD?" he quipped in return.

"Actually both," she replied, "but most people know me as Kathryn Stafford."

"Well, Kathryn Stafford, I'm Dan Fromm and I was just on my way to get a late lunch. Care to join me? No strings attached, just good conversation." Fromm pointed out the window toward the street.

She was hungry and conversation with a paleontologist might be interesting. Besides, he was nice to look at, and she loved his smile. "I'm ready for lunch," she replied.

"Great! There's a good little Italian restaurant down on Main, just across and down the block from Prairies Edge. Like Italian?"

"Love it, why don't we meet there in about 20 minutes," she said, hoping to find a few moments to reconstruct her windblown hair and freshen her makeup.

The restaurant was a welcome change from the small cafes she had been frequenting lately. It offered a quiet atmosphere and a nice Italian menu. For the first time since she had arrived, she thought about how much she was beginning to miss Miami and the creature comforts it offered.

Dan Fromm was the resident paleontologist and curator of the geological and paleontology museum at the University of Pennsylvania. He was presenting a lecture series at SDSM&T on museum management, and had been in South Dakota for almost a month. A portion of that time had been spent at the university's dig sites east of Rapid City. Kathryn shared her background with him, including the fact that she was a South Dakota native. She also told him she was currently working on a murder investigation, but stopped short of tying the investigation to her research at the college library. As they topped off lunch with a cappuccino, a middle-aged man with a gray beard approached their booth, the same man Kate had seen talking to Sam Pickens at the City Club!

"Why Dr. Fromm, I didn't know you were in town," the bearded man exclaimed. Kate' hair was worn down today and it had been dark in the Club when she had arrived that night. She hoped he didn't recognize her.

"Hey, Warren. Yes I've been here for about a month, doing my lecture series again. Warren, I'd like you to meet Kathryn Stafford. We're just shooting the breeze over desert. Care to join us?"

"No, I've got a meeting in 10 minutes. Why don't you stop by my office when you have some time. We'll catch up then."

Kathryn exhaled deeply. If the man had recognized her it wasn't evident. He had seemed to pass her over in his rush to leave the restaurant.

"Who was that man?" she casually asked.

"Oh, Warren Phips is a small-time local fossil hunter. He spends a lot of time evaluating fossil sites out here; works with the college occasionally, but mostly on his own. In fact, he was involved in a scandal a few years back that rocked, excuse the pun, the paleontology community." Dan went on to explain that in the early '90s, Warren Phips was somehow connected to the discovery a fully in-tact Tyrannosaurus Rex. Nicknamed Sue, this fossil was found to be the largest and most complete Tyrannosaurus ever discovered. The discovery got real messy. It seemed that everyone involved claimed ownership of the specimen.

The researchers who excavated the site, removed, and identified the skeleton claimed they had paid the rancher $5,000 for the fossil and therefore owned it. The rancher, on the other hand, said that the money only gave the right to excavate the land and he, the rancher, owned the dinosaur. Then the Federal Government got involved, claiming the Antiquities Act of 1906 gave the government ownership of the fossil, since the land was within the boundaries of the Cheyenne Indian Reservation. Both civil and criminal charges were filed in the case.

Kate listened intently as the story unfolded. "I seem to remember hearing about this," she said. Wasn't the fossil eventually auctioned at Sotheby's? Who finally got ownership?"

"You're right, Sue was eventually auctioned for over $8 million dollars and bought by the Field Museum in Chicago. The rancher was found to be the owner of the fossil. But it was all very confusing; while the skeleton was in the ground it was judged to be real estate and the property of the U.S. government, but because it had been removed from the ground, it became personal property and was owned by the rancher. That case set a precedent that has had a profound effect on research throughout the country. A lot of significant work has been put on hold because of it."

After agreeing to meet Dan Fromm again for dinner before he returned to Pennsylvania, Kathryn sped east toward Dupree, certain that she held the key to Wesley Johnson's murder. All for economic gain, she thought. Science again took a secondary role to profits, and in this case, murder may have also been part of the cost of the profit taking.

Who, then, were the suspects in this case? Certainly Sam Pickens must have played a key role. How had Wesley Johnson been involved? Kathryn thought that he probably had been an innocent observer, and was killed because he had seen the operation. How deeply Warren Phips was involved in the scheme and the murder was debatable, but she felt certain that he had played a role in the fossil's discovery. And what about the cowboy she had seen with Phips and Pickens at the City Club? She must ask her lab to continue enhancement of the dig site photos in hopes of a positive identification of both the people and the trailer. She would ask Mark Uses-Knives to do background checks on the suspects.

Chapter Ten

A Search By Full Moon

By the time Kathryn arrived, Sue was home and in the process of making her supper. "I've got hamburgers and fried potatoes cooking. Want some?" Sue asked. "Your fax machine has been cranking out messages since I got here, and John said to call when you got in."

"Yes, I'd like some dinner," Kathryn replied as she walked to the living room to retrieve her messages. She tore off copies of the lab reports from Miami as she dialed John's number. John updated her on the investigating team's progress at the dig site, and asked her to prepare for a meeting with members of the tribal law enforcement team the next morning.

She in turn, updated him on her findings in Rapid City, and the two agreed to focus the investigation on Sam Pickens and those potentially involved in fossil recovery. By the end of the conversation, they had formulated a plan to expand the investigation. Kathryn then asked, "John, do you think you and I could get a closer look at Pickens' horse trailer? If we find anything in the trailer connected to the dig sight, Mark Uses-Knives can get a warrant to search the entire ranch."

"Well, if we go out there it will have to be at night, and we'll need to get on the property without anyone seeing us. I guess we can do that."

"Good, there's a full moon. Can we go tonight?" she asked.

John was somewhat apprehensive about sneaking about the property without first putting a plan in place, but he agreed to make the trip if only to survey access to the ranch. "I'm not sure we'll get to see the trailer tonight, but I'm willing to at least nose around the ranch a bit. We'll have to leave late, like about 2:00 am. That OK with you?"

"You're on," Kate replied. "I'll meet you at your house."

She returned to the kitchen where Sue was eating. "Hey, Sue," Kate said as she joined her at the table, "how would you like to join us on a little field trip tonight?"

"God, do you two work all the time? I got a day job, ya know. So, where are we going?" It was obvious that although Sue wasn't getting paid for her help, she found the project challenging and wanted to be a part of it. There was just enough danger to make it interesting and considerably more exciting than patrolling the government pasture.

When Kathryn explained what they planned to do that evening, Susan's eyes widened and shaking her head, she exclaimed, "You guys are crazy, you know? What happens if we get caught out there?"

"I was hoping that you would prevent that from happening," Kate offered.

The women planned the late night visit, pulling together items they would need: dark clothing, gloves, flashlights, small tools, plastic bags, and a hand gun. Their objective would be to quietly enter the property, search the horse trailer for evidence, and leave. After stacking their gear at the front door, they hoped to grab a few hours sleep before leaving.

Just before 2:00 am, the two women emerged, dressed in jeans, dark shirts and dark jackets. They laughed as they looked at one another. "God, we look like somebody out of the movies! That's what this feels like, like we're in this old movie about to meet up with the bad guys," Sue said.

"Let's just hope we don't meet up with the bad guys, lady!" Kate responded. "I can't come up with any logical explanation of why we're out there if we get caught. And it would probably screw up the whole case. Please, let's just not get caught!"

"You ladies are looking your finest!" said John as he climbed into the Jeep. Kate and Susan began laughing again as they surveyed John's clothing. Like them, he was dressed in black. "The Guns of Navarone is what comes to mind," stated Kate. "What do you think?"

"Yup, that works for me," replied Sue watching John's puzzled reaction the comment.

It took about a half hour to reach the Flying W Ranch. They parked behind some bushes at the closest section line road, and decided to walk in from the side rather than use the main entrance. Kate put on the back pack she had loaded, and John grabbed a flash light and his Winchester rifle. The sky was filled with a light cloud cover, just enough to protect their profiles from a bright full moon. They crossed over the barbed wire fence and moved quietly across the pasture.

"Do you know if they have a dog?" asked Sue.

"I didn't see one when we were out here the other day, but that doesn't mean there isn't one," said John.

"Well, just in case, I brought this," Sue said, showing them the left over hamburger meat from supper. "And this", she pulled a juicy bone from her pocket.

"Christ, Sue, you're going to have every wild animal out here chasing us!" exclaimed John.

"Maybe, but it sure is a good idea. I'd rather have a dog happy than ripping our legs off," Kathryn added.

From a distance they could see a yard light shining brightly in between the house and the barn yard. It allowed them to locate the whereabouts of the trailer before entering the yard. Fortunately the trailer was on the far side of the barn, next to the loading shoots. With the protection of the corrals and barn between the trailer and the ranch house, it would be considerably easier to make their search without being seen or heard. They decided to place Sue within sight of both the ranch house and the horse trailer. She would be the lookout for any activity from the house.

John stealthily crept up to the trailer, searching for a side entry door while Kathryn examined the wheels and proceeded to paint a textured rubber material on the tires. When it dried, she would peel the material off the tires and have a reliable imprint of the tread markings.

Having found an unlocked side door, John gently pulled up on the latch and opened it. Suddenly, they heard a pounding noise from the coral next to them, then the sound of galloping hoofs and a loud whinny. They froze, staring at one another, as the horses continued to whinny and gallop around the coral. Moments later, they heard a quiet whisper as Sue crawled through the grass toward them.

"Lights on in the house," she murmured. "Get in the trailer and I'll lay still over in that grass. I'll come back for you when it's clear. Don't move until then."

John and Kate crawled into the trailer and waited. Sue edged her way back until she could see the house. She watched as someone walked through the yard toward the corral. Another light switched on, illuminating the corral and barn, and the horses trotted over to a figure standing at the gate. Susan could hear her heart beating as she waited in the deep grass. "Oh damn," she thought. "I just hope we can get out of here before someone finds us." Just then, the lighted corral became dark. She watched as the man returned across the yard to the door and waited until she saw the lights go off in the house. Making her way back to the trailer, she softly tapped on the door. "They're gone," she whispered. "Will you guys please hurry so we can get out of here!"

Kate quickly moved the tiny flashlight beam along the edges of the trailer. The floor had a wood base covered with straw. In one corner, a rock was lodged under the floor plank, lifting it slightly from the floor. She shined the light directly on the board and looked through the crack. "Can you pry this board up a bit, John, so I can get a closer look," she asked. As he lifted the plank, she shined the flashlight below it. Under the floor of the trailer, it appeared that there was a subfloor, creating a container under the full length of the trailer. It was about 12 inches deep. She looked at John and commented, "I've seen this before. They use false floors like this to smuggle drugs. Lets see of there's anything inside." She shined the light into the container, then reached back inside to recover an object. What she pulled out looked like a small piece of plaster with a sheet of toilet tissue attached to it. She placed it in her bag along with a clump of dirt from the cavity. They then surveyed the underside of the trailer, observing how well the subfloor had been camouflaged within the structure of the side walls — a very professional job.

"Let's get out of here," John said, helping to remove the last pieces of plastic mold from the tire. They made their way through the grass to

Susan and quietly left the ranch. By the time they reached the truck, everyone seemed to be coming down from an adrenaline rush.

Sue took a deep breath of night air and exclaimed, "Boy, am I glad that's done! I wouldn't make a very good stake-out officer."

"Speaking of stake, would you please get rid of that hamburger and the bone. You'll be smelling up the truck all the way home," John replied.

"No, I want to give it to my dogs," she protested.

With that, Kate reached into her backpack and pulled out a large plastic bag. "Here, put it in the bag. That should keep everybody happy. Now lets get home before the sun rises."

Kate smiled as she thought about a night, many years ago, when she and John were racing to return home before the sun rose. They had gone with a group of local teens to a dance in Faith. She wasn't supposed to go to out-of-town dances, but she had pleaded with John to take her along. When they got to the dance, a fight broke out between the White and Indian teenagers. John got caught in the middle of the scuffle and when the town sheriff arrived, he didn't wait to listen for explanations. All the Indian teens involved were transported to the police station.

"Hey John, remember in high school when we went to the dance in Faith and you got caught up in the fight and went to jail?" Kate asked.

"Sure do, and if it hadn't been for you telling the sheriff I was with you and had nothing to do with the fight, I would have stayed in jail. It was just about this time of morning when we got home. I remember being scared that if we got home after sun-up your parents would not respect me and never let you see me again. I didn't let you tag along after that, remember?"

Sue watched the two as they talked about the past. She could see the love they had for one another, and was beginning to understand the bond between her Indian friend and the city girl who seemed so different from them. Perhaps she wasn't so different as Sue had imagined. They had all shared the same small-town experience, with its prejudice and double standards. Kathryn had left it all behind when she went away, but she hadn't forgotten those days and the way things were.

"So, what's the significance of a piece of plaster in the trailer?" John asked, attempting to avoid the uncomfortable memories of his youth when he wasn't John Redbull, BIA agent, but just another one of those "shiftless" Indian kids, causing trouble in the town.

"I'm not sure, but I intend to call someone who might know the answer," said Kate, thinking of her new friend, Dan Fromm, in Rapid City. She was certain, however, that they would soon have enough evidence to warrant searching the Flying W property. It was also time for Sam Pickens to begin answering some tough questions.

Chapter Eleven

The Bombing

At 9:00 am the next morning, Kathryn placed a call to the Geology Department of the South Dakota School of Mines. She asked Dr. Dan Fromm if plaster was used in any way in paleontology research.

"Of course," he replied. "we use it all the time in transporting fossils, especially dinosaur bones. We usually wrap the bones thoroughly in tissue paper and then place a plaster cast around it to ensure nothing breaks while we're transporting. We also use it to cast pieces of bone for reconstruction. I know you haven't wanted to talk to me about why you're so interested in paleontology, but I'm really curious as to what you're up to."

"Sorry Dan, I really can't discuss it with you now, but I'll tell you about it sometime soon, OK?" Kathryn wondered about Dan Fromm. Was he a part of this case, as well? Somehow she had the feeling he was not, and she hoped she was correct. But for now, she had to regard him as and expert in his field with connections to at least one of the suspects.

"So will I see you soon?" he asked. He was fascinated with this woman, and hoped they could develop a friendship that would continue when they both returned to the East Coast. She was pretty, savvy, and a pleasure to be around. Dan Fromm hadn't felt that comfortable around a female since his wife had passed away four years ago. He didn't want to lose her.

"Of course," replied Kathryn, "you still owe me a dinner. I'll call you as soon as I'm free, and hopefully our schedules with be in sinc." Placing the phone in its cradle, she added her notes to the file and placed it atop the growing stack on her desk.

Kathryn felt confident that she had enough information for the Tribal Police to justify their expansion of the investigation. She had tied the murder victim to a probable fossil excavation site. The glue on the cane tip found at the site matched the glue on the cane that was among Johnson's personal possessions at the time of the murder. The horse trailer belonging to Sam Pickens could be confirmed through Wesley Johnson's photographs to be on the same dig site. She was also sure that the tire prints taken from the dig site would match the trailer. It's false bottom likewise suggested that materials other than horses were being transported. Finally, the connection between Pickens and the fossil hunter in Rapid City, the presence of plaster packing material in the subfloor, and the identification of fossil fragments in the death wound of the victim all tied Sam Pickens and a paleontology discovery to the crime of murder.

Kathryn and John Redbull spent the remainder of the day disclosing their findings to the Tribal Police. Plans were made to coordinate the issuance of search warrants with the local Ziebach County authorities and to organize a law enforcement team to conduct the search. With the exception of few loose ends, they were also close to issuing an arrest warrant for Pickens.

Kathryn arrived home early that afternoon, the first time in days that she had had an opportunity to relax. She planned to catch up on some personal phone calls, and maybe re-establish her life back in Miami. Her dog was being cared for by friends, and she missed him terribly. She had missed the most important fund-raiser of the season, an awards dinner supporting youth services in Dade County, and annual women's sailing regatta was to be held this weekend. She was certain her friends thought she had fallen from the face of the earth. And they weren't far from the truth, she thought.

She slipped into a comfortable jogging suit and gathered logs from the back of the house. Tonight, she vowed, would be quiet and peaceful — crackling logs on the fire, some good music, and the book she had been reading on the airplane. As she prepared for the evening, it suddenly occurred to her that during all of time she had been in South Dakota, she hadn't once thought about her family. Thinking it odd that she had spent almost two weeks in the area and had not found the time to visit the family ranch or to look up old friends and neighbors, Kathryn's demeanor saddened. She knew that she hadn't been able to bring herself to the realization that it was all gone, a part of her past. This was the reason she hadn't returned home in over ten years. Home didn't exist here anymore she thought. The only direct connection to her past was John, and spending time with him, even in a work situation, was her tie to the past. He had been there for her when her parents were killed in the auto accident. She knew he was always there for her, even when they didn't communicate for years. He had told her at the funeral that even though her parents were gone she would always have him as family to come home to.

She remembered when she was a little girl, that John who was only three years older, had adopted her. When they attended the one-room school house near their homes, John had looked out for her, walked her home from school, kept her warm when the bitter cold singed her nose and made her toes tingle. He had loved the small girl. Even in high school, he watched over her. Aggravating as it was at times, her surrogate big brother monitored her dates and chastised her driving habits. When he left for college in her junior year, she missed him terribly, so he made an effort to bring her to campus for special occasions. She had been so proud of him then. He was her role model and she could hardly wait for her own college days to begin. So it was no wonder that she and John considered each other family. When Kathryn's mother and father were killed, it was if John had lost his own parents in the senseless tragedy.

Kathryn's parents were returning home from a nearby town on a winter night eleven years ago. The roads were slick and the visibility poor. Her father had attempted to brake at a stop sign, but the car went into a skid, stopping in the path of an oncoming tractor-trailer. They were killed instantly. Kathryn came home for the funeral, settled their affairs, and sold the ranch. Then she returned to Miami and resumed her life. She remembered an emptiness then, but had never taken the time to acknowledge it nor to mourn for her parents. Before leaving here she knew that she must face the tragedy and say a proper goodbye to her their memory.

The sound of dogs barking promptly brought Kathryn back to the present. She looked up to see Sue standing in the doorway. She had almost forgotten that Sue was still staying at the cottage but was actually relieved to see another human being. After a brief recap of their respective work days, the two decided they deserved to eat out. Was it to be the City Club or Buster's Cafe? They opted for Busters.

Over supper they talked about life in Dupree and Miami. Sue was curious about what it was like to live in a big city, although she said she had no desire to ever live in one. She also wanted to know about the ocean, and did Kathryn sail and dive and all of the things she had watched people do on TV. Kathryn wanted to know why Susan stayed in Dupree and if she had ever wanted to live, or even visit, anywhere else. Miami would definitely be an eye-opener for her, Kathryn surmised, but not necessarily a positive experience. She recalled her first experiences with city life. The traffic was terrifying and the close proximity to many people was suffocating. The most difficult adjustment, however, was the presence of constant noise; traffic, sirens, construction — all sounds that were foreign to her. She remembered not being able to sleep because of the noise. Now, she found the quiet of the prairie disconcerting. The absence of sound was frightening.

The two women talked about Kate's plan to build a cabin somewhere out on the prairie. Sue knew of a few locations that might provide the perfect setting and promised to keep her eye out for available parcels of land. They both decided it would be fun to do some riding and fishing in the upcoming summers. Sue offered to help Kathryn build the cabin and to board a horse for her while she was away. A nice friendship was developing between the two, and Kate looked forward to their summer adventures.

Kathryn and Susan arrived home at about 8:30. Kathryn rekindled the fire in the fireplace, and Sue fed her dogs. As Kate was leaning over to stoke the fire, she heard a sudden crash behind her. Swinging around, she felt a blast of air and saw flames in the middle of the living room!

"What the hell was that?" cried Sue running from the kitchen.

"A fire bomb!" screamed Kathryn.

Sue was already on her way out the door. She ran back with a large fire extinguisher and yelled, "Here, put out the fire with this. I'm going after the son of a bitch!"

Kathryn extinguished the fire quickly. Fast thinking on Sue's part had prevented it from becoming a serious blaze. Picking up the phone as she caught her breath, Kate dialed John's number. "John, we were just firebombed at the house! They may be headed your way. Sue is chasing them now...no, everything is OK here, just a broken window." She hung up the phone, still shaking. "Coffee," she thought, "do I need a cup of coffee!"

Not yet in the kitchen, the phone rang and Kate turned to answer it. "Kate, its Sue. I'm at the police station, and I've got him. Can you come down?"

"I'm calling John, then I'm on my way," was the reply.

When she and John arrived at the station, they found Sue sitting with the policeman and a young cowboy. "This here's Rodney Rassmussen," stated the Chief of Police. "Seems he's in a whole lot a trouble tonight."

"Rodney?" said John, amazed that the boy could be involved in all of this. Rodney was JR's age and the son of Sam Rassmussen. "What the hell have you been doing? Have they called your father?"

"No, no, please don't call my father. He doesn't know anything about this. I'm sorry, John, I'm so sorry about the whole thing." Rodney Rassmussen's body trembled as he looked up at John like a frightened puppy.

"Who put you up to this?" John demanded.

"I can't say. Honest, I can say!" replied the boy.

"Rodney, I know you're not a bad kid. I've known you all your life. But this is serious trouble you've gotten yourself into, and you must tell us who put you up to it."

Sue stood over the boy. "Kid, I'm not a cop so I don't have to obey cop rules. You just firebombed the house I'm staying in, and I want to know why or I'm going to beat the holy shit out of you! Understand?"

"I got to have some protection before I say anything," Rodney retorted. "If I talk, they'll kill me, I know they will."

"Rodney, as of now, you are under U.S. government protection. I promise. Now, can I call your father and have him arrange to get a lawyer for you. You're going to need one, young man," John stated.

Young Rassmussen finally agreed to contact his father and to hire the services of a lawyer. "I ain't leaving this jail, though, and I ain't even going to stay in here by myself. Too dangerous!"

John had this kid exactly where he wanted him. If he stayed scared, he would probably talk. And John believed he held most of the answers to the Johnson crime. After talking to his father, it was agreed that Rodney Rassmussen would remain in jail overnight. A lawyer, both the local and Tribal Police, and the investigating team would be present at his questioning tomorrow. If they were lucky, the boy would lead them to the suspects and offer a motive for the murder.

Chapter Twelve

The Interrogation

Rodney Rassmussen sat in a small room in the Ziebach County Courthouse. His father, Sam Rassmussen, sat to his left, and his lawyer, an older man in a dark brown suit and an agate bolo tie, sat to the boy's right. The interrogating team consisted of the Dupree Chief of Police, Mark Uses-Knives representing the Tribal Police, John Redbull, Kathryn Stafford, and a recording clerk.

Police Chief Morgan stood. "Mr. Rassmussen, you are here this morning to answer questions pertaining to the attempted fire bombing of a residence at 216 Second Avenue West in Dupree. You have been given your rights and have a lawyer present. Do you have any questions before we begin?"

"No sir," replied the boy.

The Chief continued, "Your name is Rodney Allen Rassmussen, you are 19 years of age, and you reside on your parent's ranch 14 miles southwest of Dupree. Correct?"

"Yes sir."

"Rodney, at approximately 9:15 last night did you throw a flaming bottle of gasoline through the front window of the residence at 216 Second Avenue West?"

Rodney: "I did."

Chief: "Was anyone else with you when you did this?"

Rodney: "No, I was alone."

Chief: "Why did you throw the bottle through the window of this house."

Rodney: "It was to scare the lady staying at the house."

Chief: "And why did you want to scare this lady? Did you know her?

Rodney: "No sir, I did not. She was nosing around into some affairs around here, and certain people wanted her to leave town. They thought if she was scared enough she would leave."

Chief: "Are these the same people who sent her a threatening letter three days ago?"

Rodney: "Yes."

Chief: "And did you deliver that letter to this same house?"

Rodney: Looking at his lawyer, the two conversed briefly. "Yes."

Chief: "And can you tell me who asked you to deliver the letter and fire bomb to this residence?"

Rodney: "I cannot sir, until you guarantee me that I will have some protection. John Redbull said last night that the government would protect me if I gave names."

Chief: "I'm afraid I'm not in a position to offer you U.S. government protection, son. This crime was committed here in Dupree, not on the reservation."

Uses-Knives: "I am, however, authorized to offer Mr. Rassmussen Cheyenne Tribal law enforcement security. We think he has pertinent information about a case we are working on, and it is believed that his actions in the two times committed in Dupree are directly connected to our case. Further, it is our opinion that any information given by this individual to authorities would place him in grave danger."

It was evident that jurisdictional issues prevented continued questioning. Chief Morgan, Mark Uses-Knives, John Redbull, and Rassmussen's lawyer adjourned to the City Attorney's office to resolve the question of police protection. On the way out of the court house, John and Mark Uses-Knives asked Kathryn to put the tribal officers on alert. They were to post a team outside the Flying W Ranch to prevent anyone from leaving; holding them for questioning, if necessary. They were to also engage the assistance of the South Dakota Hiway Patrol in ensuring that Pickens did not escape.

The issue of police protection was resolved quickly. Everyone involved in the case recognized the urgency of obtaining young Rassmussen's confession. Others implicated in the crime were likely to take some action when they realized he had been arrested.

Chapter Thirteen

Rodney Rassmussen

Rodney Rassmussen had always been a good kid. Everyone liked him. He had done well in high school, played on the varsity football and basketball teams and served on the student counsel. He was artistically inclined, found drafting and art to be his favorite classes, and designed the school's team mascot, a characterized bison wearing the jersey of the home team and twirling a lassoo. His teachers felt he had great potential, and were therefore surprised when he decided not to attend college. They were not of aware of the role that Rodney's father had played in that decision.

Sam Rassmussen had inherited the family ranch. The Rassmussens had been sheep ranchers since Sam's grandfather had staked a homestead south of Dupree in the early 1900s. Sam took pride in the fact that, while other farmers and ranchers in the area had succumbed to bankruptcy brought on by low prices and high operating costs, he had survived. In fact, the Rassmussen ranch was quite profitable due to Sam's careful management and no-frills approach. Sam knew that his only son, Rodney, would become the fourth generation to run the operation that he and his father and grandfather had built. So when Rodney approached his father with plans to attend college and major in art and design, Sam's dreams for the ranch's future were shattered. His response to the boy dashed any hopes Rodney may have had about leaving. If Rodney chose to leave, Sam had said, then he would do so with no help from the family. Sam would provide no funds for college, and moreover, Rodney would be disinherited and no longer welcome at home.

Rodney was stunned by his father's response. He felt trapped into a lifestyle that didn't fit him. He hated sheep, hated the lonely summers he had spent herding them, hated the spring shearing season when his back and hands were sore from cutting and bundling the wool from hundreds of animals. His father couldn't understand that the boy had hopes and dreams of his own, not unlike his father's dreams for building the ranch.

After months of pleading and with the welcomed support of his mother, Rodney finally convinced his father to allow him to get a local job as a cowhand. The father rationalized that becoming 'hired help' would soon convince his son of the advantages of working on his own ranch. Rodney's motivation for working, however, was different than his father had imagined. Rodney hoped to save enough money to leave the ranch, and knowing that he could never expect to return, he would use his savings to attend school and build a career for himself. The boy took a job with Sam Pickens as a ranch hand. At the time, he was naively unaware of the devastating impact it would have on his future.

After meeting with his lawyer to review the terms of agreement for witness protection, Rodney Rassmussen was prepared to talk. The interrogation resumed.

Chief: "Mr. Rassmussen, are you now prepared to tell us who asked you to deliver the letter and gasoline bomb to Dr. Stafford's residence?"

Rodney: "Yes. (pause) It was my boss, Sam Pickens.

Chief: "And Rodney, do you know why it was so important that Dr. Stafford be frightened into leaving town?"

Rodney: "Well, she was investigating Wes Johnson's death, and Sam was afraid she would lead the police to our operation. He thought if she wasn't around, they probably would drop the investigation."

Chief: "And what was that operation, Rodney?"

Rodney: "I don't know."

Chief: "Rodney, you are in this situation up to your eyeballs. I suggest you try very hard to remember the details."

Rodney: "I'm sorry, but I don't know anything else."

It was evident that the young cowboy refused to tell them what he knew about the crime. He had identified Sam Pickens as the originator of the threatening note and the firebomb, thereby implicating him in Johnson's murder as well. But they still lacked a motive. They did, however, have enough information to arrest Pickens. Mark Uses-Knives immediately left the room, presumably to notify his officers to issue the arrest warrant.

Kathryn decided that if she were to present Rodney Rassmussen with the evidence she currently held, it may persuade him to fill in the details. She asked Chief Morgan if it were possible for her to interrogate him. He agreed.

Kathryn opened her questioning by asking if Rodney knew how much evidence she had acquired pertaining to Wes Johnson's death.

Rodney: "No, I just knew you were looking into it."

Stafford: "Well Rodney, I think you should know about some of the facts we have. If you have any information to add to what we already know, it will help your case. If you can't help us with this, you may be held as an accessory to murder. In addition, with the information we already have, Pickens is going to believe that you have given us these details. So any way you look at it, you're screwed. And that police protection you were offered is likely to be withdrawn if you can't cooperate with us. Now, let get down to the details. We know where Wes Johnson was murdered. It was on a site in the hills southeast of Pickens' ranch. On that site, the ground had been excavated for fossils which were loaded into the false bottom of Sam Pickens' horse trailer. Johnson likely came upon the operation accidentally. Oh yes, we also have photos of the operation. As we speak, those photos are being enhanced to provide a positive identification of the men involved. Need I continue? Rodney, I'm going to give you an hour to talk with your lawyer about this. I think it's in your best interest to talk to us."

It took Rodney Rassmussen only 30 minutes to respond. For the remainder of the afternoon, he gave the investigators details of a well organized plan to remove a large and very rare Triceratops from the Indian land adjoining Pickens' ranch. Pickens had discovered the fossil over a year ago. He had contacted a fossil expert in Rapid City who verified that the skeleton was a rare dinosaur which appeared to be almost perfectly preserved. Aware that they could not legally remove the fossil from government land and retain ownership, Pickens and the fossil hunter developed a plan to remove the bones from the original site and transplant them in another location. They knew that if they could claim ownership of the skeleton, it would be worth several million dollars. If the Tyronosaurus Rex, Sue, had been auctioned for $8.4 million, this fossil would surely bring few million. The young man went on to explain that he did not know where the fossil had been taken, only that his employer, Pickens had told him that if he helped with the excavation, he would receive a share of the money. Later, his participation in the scheme was used as a threat to keep him quiet about the project and about the murder.

Stafford: "Rodney, were you present at the site when Wes Johnson was killed?"

Rodney: "Yes."

Stafford: "What happened?"

Rodney: "Well, Wes worked for my dad as a sheep herder. He was a good ol' boy, really in to nature and stuff like that. Nothing would have ever happened if he hadn't been herdin' sheep on the other side of the hill. Even then, if the dumb bastard hadn't come down to the trailer while we were loading he wouldn't have got hurt. He comes down there and tells Sam he's been watching what we're doing. In fact, he says he's got pictures of it all. Says he won't take no money to be quiet, but that fossil better show up someplace like a museum for people to see."

Stafford: "What happened then?"

Rodney: "One of Sam's men comes walkin' up to take his camera, and ol' Wes starts fightin' with him, hittin' him with that cane of his. Then Sam grabs a bone he's packin' and slams him over the head with it. I don't think he really ment to kill him. So anyway, Wes was dead. We didn't know what to do with him so we ended up taking him up to a cave, hopin' nobody would ever find him. I'm so sorry it happened." Rodney began to sob. "I really liked Wes. I wanted to tell somebody, because I didn't want him just lying out there in that cave. He should've had a decent funeral with his family and all. But when I told Sam that, he told me to just keep my mouth shut or I wouldn't get any money, or worse yet, I'd be up there with him Since then, I've been doing pretty much everything he tells me. I just wanted to get my money and go to Denver t design school and never come back!"

Stafford: "Who was there when Wes was killed?"

Rodney: "Well, there was me and Sam, and that Phips fella, and a cowboy at the ranch named Charley."

Stafford: "Who else was involved in the plan to remove the fossil."

Rodney: "God, I don't know, these are the only people I ever saw at the ranch."

Stafford: "And where did they take the fossil?"

Rodney: "Someplace out in Montana. They bought some land out there, and then trailered a load of Appaloosa out with the bones. I didn't go so I don't know the location."

Later that day Rodney Rassmussen was charged with two counts of felony in Ziebach County — the two threats against Kathryn Stafford, and six federal felony counts related to the murder, its cover-up, and the removal of antiquities from federal government property. It had been agreed that, with his testimony against the others, Rassmussen would receive leniency by the courts. Rodney's father pledged to help the boy in any way that he could.

Chapter Fourteen

The Trackers

Mark Uses-Knives walked into the room as Rassmussen was being charged. He motioned to John and Kate.

"We were too late," he said sharply. "My men entered the ranch and Pickens was gone. We know he didn't leave by the road. We had it covered. And he didn't leave by a vehicle either. Nobody at the ranch is talking, but we're holding them all for questioning. My guess is he took off on horseback for the hills, probably headed southeast to the badlands. There are no roads and its hard to get a car back there. I've notified the Feds and they'll be bringing a helicopter out from Rapid to do a search."

John and Kathryn exchanged concerned glances. John replied, "What can we do to assist?"

"Just stay around here and try to collect more evidence," was Uses-Knives response.

A short time later Kate and John returned to her cottage. Neither of them were pleased with the entry of Federal authorities into the case. They knew, however, that at this stage of the search, Federal involvement was inevitable.

As Kathryn browsed her incoming messages — one from Dan Fromm asking her to call immediately, John interrupted her thoughts. "You know, Kate, no matter how many helicopters and search teams they bring in to find him, they're not going to succeed. There are too many places to hide in the badlands. This is job for trackers who know the area; its really a job for us Indians. We know where and how to search."

"Am I hearing what I think I'm hearing? You want to conduct your own search?" she asked.

"Well, there are some people who know this area real well, and I think our chances of finding him are as good or better than anyone else."

"Who do you have in mind?" Kate replied.

"Sue Badger, for one," he said. "Sue knows those hills better than anybody, except maybe Tom Crowfeather. I don't know if he's able to ride any more, but Tom used to be the best tracker around. He had a sixth sense when it came to tracking man or animal. He uses the old ways, the ways our people used to find water and hunt game before there were roads and helicopters. And then I thought maybe you and me and my son, JR."

Kathryn was taken aback. The thought of the five of them initiating a manhunt in the remote badlands seemed almost humorous to her. But she could see that John was quite serious about the idea. "I agree that having people involved who know the area would be helpful," she said thoughtfully, "but don't you think it would be more productive if you worked with the official search team and guided them to the badlands?"

"No," he answered. "We'll find him if we go in quietly and alone. Besides, it will be less dangerous if we can just sneak up and capture him."

Kate then realized that John's plan involved more than the capture of Sam Pickens. Something deeply rooted in his culture stirred within him. Using the skills of his ancestors, skills that were almost forgotten in the modern world, he could use this search party to reconnect with the past. And he wanted to share that experience with those who could understand it: Sue, who shared the heritage and the skills passed on to her by her people, Tom Crowfeather, who was part of that past and John's connection to the elders of his tribe, Kathryn, who shared his childhood, and finally, his son, the person who would carry on his cultural legacy. She suddenly felt compassion for him and both understood and shared his need to reconnect with the old ways. There was something to be gained from seeking knowledge and guidance from the land — truth based in the reality of nature, yet spiritual in content. Yes, she wanted to accompany him on his tracking quest, and perhaps rediscover her own values as well.

She knew that the helicopters with their plethora of electronic gadgetry would probably locate Sam Pickens before the tracking party, but it was to be a competition of sorts — the value of old versus new. Kathryn was sure that no matter the outcome, the horse trackers would return wiser from the experience.

The sound of the telephone ringing jolted Kathryn back to the present. She answered and heard Dan Fromm's voice. This was an inappropriate time to discuss dinner plans she thought, so she was surprised to hear the true purpose of his call.

"Kathryn, I need to discuss a conversation I had today. I think it may have some bearing on the work you are doing up there. I know you didn't tell me what your criminal case was about, but I put some facts together today and they seem to fit. If you are investigating the murder of a young man, a sheep herder, then I think I have some information you should know."

"Ah, yes, that's the case I'm working on," she replied. "We've had a big break in the case today. What do you know about all of this?"

"Well, a few days ago I met with Warren Phips. Do you remember the man we met at the restaurant? He asked me if I knew of a museum interested in buying a near-perfect Triceratops. He wanted to know if I was interested. I told him that, of course, I would be interested but doubted that I could pay the going price for such a specimen. Our museum isn't blessed with a lot of wealthy donors. So today I started hearing rumors around the college that the authorities were searching for the murderers of a young man up your way, and that it was somehow connected to a paleontology find. I started putting the facts together and suspected that this was your investigation. Then, earlier today I got another call from Phips. This time he offered me the fossil for $1.5 million if I could close the deal immediately. He said he wanted to make the exchange as soon as possible. When I inquired as to the whereabouts of the fossil, he wouldn't say. I told him that it would take some time for my foundation to come up with the funds and that's how we left it."

"Wow, yes this is directly related to our case, Dan," she said. "Would you be willing to help us?"

"Sure, what can I do?"

"I want you to contact Inspector Mark Uses-Knives in Eagle Butte. Tell him everything you just told me. Also, tell him that with their assistance, I would like you to go through with the sale. Hopefully it will lead us to the fossil. We definitely don't want Phips arrested yet. Better to wait until he makes the exchange with you."

"Got it," Fromm replied. "I'll call him now. And remember, when this is over, you owe me that dinner date."

"Sure thing," she answered, "I'll even buy dinner. And Dan, please be careful."

While they awaited Sue Badger's return to the cottage, Kate explained the details of her conversation with Dan Fromm. John was certain that Phips knew the whereabouts of Sam Pickens and would try to help him escape from the badlands. If Phips negotiated the sale of the fossil and transferred the funds out of the area, the two men could easily just disappear.

Kathryn considered the possibility that Phips knew where and how to locate Sam Pickens. If he planned to help the rancher escape, they must have some method of communication and a way to transport him out of the hills.

"John, we need to find out if Pickens has a cellular phone. If he does, Eagle Butte can track his calls. They should also put a tap on Warren Phips' telephones." She knew that they couldn't trace the location of his cell phone calls, but they would at least have a warning, should Pickens prepare to escape from the area.

Later that evening Kathryn, John, and Sue Badger discussed plans to go into the badlands. They agreed that the search party would need to get underway as soon as possible and began to prepare for the ride.

They would need an additional two pack horses, warm clothing, light camping equipment, and food supplies for at least five days.

As the two women began assembling gear, John left to notify JR and Tom Crowfeather of their plans. He wasn't sure that Crowfeather could, or would want to make the trip, but John knew that the old man's knowledge would be an immense help in the search.

Chapter Fifteen

Packing In

Bright rays of sunlight filled the eastern sky as the search party assembled along the banks of the Cheyenne River. Five saddle horses grazed quietly near the water as the team loaded sleeping bags, tents and provisions on to the pack team. John strapped his Winchester case on the saddle and stored a box of 30-30 shells in the saddlebag. Both he and JR wore long waterproof slickers, cut up the back allowing the coattails to fall freely along the sides of the saddle. Old Crowfeather rode a stocky bay mare, loaded with his bedroll, full saddle bags, a lariat, and a World War II single shot army rifle.

Kate smiled as she watched three generations of plains- men prepare for the ride. She quietly pulled her camera from its case and focused on the staging area. Sue was wearing a white Pendleton trapper's coat with stripes along the shoulders, Tom wore his black felt hat with a red feather, and the father and son, their long riding coats and oversized cowboy hats. Some pictures were timeless; set in the 1890s or the year 2000, the characters remained unchanged.

"Riders, mount up," yelled John Redbull, and the search party slowly moved in the direction of the rising sun.

Two hours into the journey, the riders dismounted to rest the horses and survey the landscape. Tom Crowfeather spoke. "If he came from over there," he said, pointing north, "then he would stop somewhere along the river here to water his horse. Then he would go this way along the river bank. We will see his tracks."

As they continued to ride east, the river gradually widened, carrying the backflow of the Oahe Reservoir, modern man's success in harnessing the power of the Missouri River 60 miles downstream. The barren tops of long-dead cottonwood trees were still visible in the water, and the river's flow began to slow as its banks widened.

The lead horse stopped suddenly, and Sue called to the older man. "This is what you're looking for, Tom," she said, looking down at the tracks along the bank."

As the riders dismounted to examine the tracks, they heard the shrill cry of a bird. Looking up, they saw a large hawk-like bird circling above.

"That's an eagle," exclaimed Sue.

"A very good sign," replied Crowfeather. "It means that the Great One has sent the eagle from *Wanbli oyate* (the Eagle nation) to watch over us and show us the way. The eagle can see great distances. He will help us in our search. If he stays with us, we have great power. We are fortunate to be riding the trail of the eagle."

The tracks along the riverbank indicated that a man and horse had stopped there. The horse was unshod, and judging from the strand of hair attached to a branch near the water, it had the light brown main or tail characteristic of a light colored appaloosa. A dung heap left behind was fresh, less than a day or two old. The tracks continued southeast beside the river. They followed the tracks downstream, and when the sun began to decend in the western sky, it was time to search for a place to rest for the night.

Sue choose a camp site at a bend in the river. There, the river was shallow and the gradual sloping banks were protected by a towering cliff to the north. The cliff offered protection from the north wind, while the meadow below provided grazing space for the animals. The group unsaddled the horses and erected a temporary corral for the remuda. This was done by stretching ropes around several large cottonwood trees to form an enclosure.

JR and John began to set up the tents in a large circle around what was to become the communal camp fire, while Sue and Kate searched for logs for the fire. The old man gathered a pouch from his bedroll and slowly walked downstream and out of site.

"Where's that old man going?" asked JR. "Shouldn't somebody go with him? He's so old he might get lost."

John grabbed JR's shoulder firmly. "Don't you worry about old Tom," he said. "Did you see the bag he was carrying? It's his medicine bag. He is going off by himself to seek *taku wakan* (the sacred things) and to speak to the *wahutopa* "four-leggeds" about our search. You can learn much from him JR, so watch and listen to what he has to say."

Kathryn reclined on her opened sleeping bag and rested her head on the seat of her saddle. She could hear the water rippling over river stones and the sound of rustling cottonwood leaves. The sounds faded gradually as she closed her eyes and drifted into a peaceful sleep.

When she awoke, she looked up to see Sue leaning over the flames of the campfire. "Oh, how long have I been asleep?" she asked.

"Bout long enough for me to get this fire started without your help," Sue retorted. "Your gonna get dish duty for that! Come with me to find more logs. We'll need to keep the fire burning steady all night just to keep warm."

As they walked along the river looking for dry wood, Kate looked at Susan, thinking that this was a woman of both worlds, accustomed to modern living but equally comfortable with the old ways. "Sue," she said. "Do you believe in the spirit life of your people, I mean *wankan tanka* and speaking with the "four-leggeds"?"

"Oh, absolutely" replied Sue. "I not only believe it, I use it. We are all part of God's universe — the plants, the animals, and you and me. God speaks through nature if you just take time to listen. John tells me that he thinks you have lost your soul. You can no longer read the messages, because you have lived too long in the city. He thinks you need to regain your balance. Do you think this is true?"

"Well, yes maybe," Kate said pensively. Was it so obvious that she lost the ability to be at peace with herself?

"John wants you and JR learn from this journey, and for you to maybe find your soul again. He believes that riding the trail of the eagles will give both of you wisdom and strength."

"That's damn interesting," Kathryn exclaimed, "and I thought we were out here looking for a killer, not my soul!"

"Don't be upset with him, Kate. He just wants good things for you, just like he does for JR. He maybe sees things about you that you can't see for yourself," Sue said.

"I know, and I'm sorry if I seem angry with him. He's right, I could use more balance in my life, and more connection with the world around me. It seems like work and my immediate life are the only things important to me right now. And I suppose there is much more of value out there that I'm not experiencing. I do know that I'm very comfortable out here. It's a part of my life that I've missed very much."

"Then maybe you are finding your soul again." Sue smiled at her and bent over to pick up a branch from a fallen tree.

Chapter Sixteen

Wankan Tanka

After supper, the group gathered by the fire. Kathryn pulled the sheepskin collar of her bomber jacket tightly around her ears. Tom Crowfeather was wrapped in a woolen, beaver pattern robe. The logs crackled, spitting shots of flame into the air. It was almost May, and the chance of the temperature dropping to below freezing was remote. Nonetheless, it was a cold tonight and the air was crisp. A blanket if stars filled the sky. Tom pulled a long pipe from inside his robe and began to speak.

"We should smoke the pipe tonight," he said, "and ask the spirits of our ancestors to guide us in the morning. I have spoken with the meadowlark, and she tells me many things that we should know. I will share them with you after we share the pipe."

Crowfeather held the pipe up to the heavens as an offering to Wankan Tanka. It was passed clockwise to each member of the party. When the ceremony was finished, the old man cleaned out the pipe and placed it in its bag. He then began his story. He told of how his people were Oglala, meaning "they scatter their own", of the Night Cloud Band. His father was a wankan person, a spiritual leader of the camp, and one of the Wolf Cult, adept at removing arrows from braves and making strong medicine against their enemies. By the time Tom was born, the Night Cloud Band had been well integrated into Oglala reservation life, and the practices of shamans and holy people were quietly practiced, but hidden from the white man. Tom, like other Indian children of the era, was taken from the family and placed at the agency boarding school, where he learned English and was taught through the eighth grade. Summers were spent with his family. His father taught him the ways of the Night Cloud Band and was proud of Tom's ability to communicate with the "four-leggeds". Throughout his life, Tom maintained communication with the animals, and tonight he would share with the trackers the message given him by the meadowlark.

Kathryn sat by the fire in awe of Tom Crowfeather's words. She had been raised with these people, and yet she was never aware that they continued to practice the old spiritual rituals. She had known of the Sun Dance, the Ghost Dance and other ceremonies of the old days, but until the 1970s, not much was said about the practices that still existed among the tribe. She was only beginning to realize the importance these religious beliefs played in the lives of the Oglala. Here, in the 21st Century, an old man was calling upon Oglala spirit guides to assist the tracking party in finding a killer.

Tom Crowfeather talked with a quiet voice in the slow measured speech of a shaman. "Today I went to the meadowlark, asking her for knowledge about the man we are seeking. She told me this was a bad man. She said he was a frightened man, and frightened men often do not consider the harm they do to others. They only react to their own fears. This makes him very dangerous to the "two-leggeds". She told me that this man will be hiding underground like the prairie dog. He can pop his head above the ground to see us, but we cannot see him. She said the man must be distracted with fear in his eyes, so that he cannot see us when we capture him. The meadowlark told me to rely on the animals to create fear in the man. Then the "two-leggeds" will take him."

"Tom," John inquired, "did she tell you where to find this underground hideout? There's a lot of badlands out there."

Crowfeather replied, "No, she said if we listen to the "four-leggeds", they will show us the way."

Sue, who had remained silent most of the evening, eagerly added, "I'm sure the animals will lead us to him. We just need to listen to the signs. But aside from that, I have an idea where to begin our search.

Deep in the ravines there is a dugout house where a hermit used to live. Back in the '20s and '30s there used to be a lot of old hermits in this country. They dug their houses into the side of a hill where it was warm and well protected. They just wanted to stay away from people, I guess. Anyway, if that dugout is still there, it would be a good place for Pickens to hide."

"I agree," said John. "Can you find the place?"

"I think so," Sue replied. "I was out there when I was a kid and stayed in the place a couple of nights. From here it's about a half day ride. We need to be very careful as we approach though, because the front of the dugout has more than a 180 view of the landscape. It's like the meadowlark said, he can pop up and see us, but we can't see him."

It was decided that the next morning they would head in to the badlands in the direction of the hermit's cave. As they approached the site, Sue would ride ahead to find the exact location and look for signs of inhabitants. They could then plan an approach to the hideout.

Kathryn listened as the team planned tomorrow's search. Usually she would have presented some ideas and participated in planning the operation. Tonight, however, she had nothing to say. As she sat by the fire with the Indian search party, she felt oddly out of place. There were no topographical maps, no heat sensing devices, no helicopters, ATVs and voice communication command posts; only four Indian guides with firsthand knowledge of the terrain and a talking bird to guide them! She wanted to believe in their ways, yet found it terribly difficult to yield rational thought to spiritual trust. Years of training had taught her to seek scientific truth. Now she was being asked to place both her safety and her faith in primitive spirituality. And although she lacked confidence in the whole idea that spirit guides and animals would lead them to the suspect, she was not uncomfortable with her surroundings. Somehow, the presence of these people, her old and new friends, made her feel secure and confident about the outcome of their journey.

As she nestled into her sleeping bag, Kathryn could feel the warmth of the crackling campfire. In the distance, she could hear the mournful howling of coyotes and she wondered if they, too, were conversing about the search for Sam Pickens.

Chapter Seventeen

Guided by the "Four-Leggeds"

Breakfast at the campsite consisted of fried egg sandwiches with ham, rawfried potatoes, and strong black coffee. Everyone seemed in good spirits as they began to break camp and repack the horses. Tom Crowfeather once again left the campsite, presumably to speak with his spirit guides. Suddenly the quiet sounds of cottonwood leaves and rippling water was overshadowed by a distant thunder. In the distance, they could see an approaching helicopter. It was following the river, headed in an easterly direction.

"Looks like the Bureau is out early this morning," said John. "Hey, Kate, you still carrying that cell phone? Maybe we could call in and ask how they're doing."

John placed a call to the Tribal Police in Eagle Butte. They had searched the area by helicopter the day before and were resuming the search this morning. So far, that had found no trace of the suspect. Kathryn inquired as to whether Phips had made contact with Sam Pickens' cellular and was told that two calls had been identified — one the day of Pickens disappearance and another yesterday morning. She was concerned that an attempt to rescue Pickens was underway. They must locate him before he fled the area. If he escaped the badlands, his apprehension would be difficult. "I hope Tom's spirit bird is talkative this morning," she thought. "We need all the help we can get!"

Today they would move inland from the river. Following a large ravine up from the water, they began to look for signs of the lone rider. The terrain became more barren as they moved further into the hills. Hundreds of years of erosion had created the corrugated hillsides and gumbo flatlands of the badlands. Layers of soil deposits were visible on the hillsides. Grass and sage grew in clumps along the sides, with small grassland mesas atop some of the larger knolls. A small herd of pronghorn antelope bounced up from their hiding place behind a patch of tall sage. Rabbits, red fox, and hawks could occasionally be seen scurrying in pursuit of prey. Inhospitable as it was to humans, the badlands offered a plentiful food supply and safety for wildlife.

As they moved deeper into the badlands, reference points began to disappear. Heavy shadows cast by the sun provided minimal direction, and it was easy to see why so many settlers and cowboys had wandered into the badlands, only to become lost and never return. Sue, however, seemed to be at home in the area, familiar with the gullies and mesas that would hopefully lead the trackers to the hermit's dugout. For hours they traveled through the washouts and across crested buttes. JR, finally tiring of the slow pace and lack of orientation, shouted, "Say, old man, are you getting any signs from the animals yet? I think we're getting lost in here."

"Son, you have not learned the patience of your elders. You tell me if you see any signs. Look around you. What do you hear? What do you see?"

"I see a lot of bare ravines leading to nowhere. I hear wind and birds," the boy replied.

"And what do they tell you?" asked the old man.

"Only that I'm hungry and need a sandwich," quipped JR.

"Yes, I know a young man sometimes cannot think when he's hungry, but if you were on a vision quest you would not have eaten for days. That's when the spirits would begin to talk to you. A strong young man such as you should do a vision quest to understand his purpose in life. He should do the Sun Dance, too, to prove he is ready for a man's responsibility. But for now, we should teach you to understand the signs of the badlands. First, which way does the wind blow?" asked Crowfeather.

"From that way," JR pointed.

"And this time of year, in the spring, is the wind warm or cold?" the old man questioned.

"Sometimes warm and sometimes cold." was the answer.

"Today, is the wind warm or cold?

"Warm?" asked the boy.

"Yes, that means it is a Chinook wind, and these warm winds usually blow from the southeast. So what direction are we traveling?" inquired Tom.

JR thought a moment and responded, "I think we are going northeast because the wind is behind us on the right side."

"Good, JR. Now, what kind of sounds are the birds making, are they screaming or are they just calling?"

"Calling, I guess, except for the hawk who screamed," JR replied.

"So the birds do not scream because they are not afraid. There is nothing here to frighten them. But the hawk screamed either because he was attacking prey or because he saw us and was unhappy we were here. Now, as you ride, look for more signs."

John watched his son and the old man as they rode together, motioning to one another about the wind, the sky, and the rocks below. He had wanted for JR to have this knowledge and to gain respect for the elders of his tribe. JR had been raised White, and John had considered this a good thing. It would give JR more opportunities in outside world. Sometimes he thought that without the stigma of Indian culture, his son would develop higher self esteem and be able to compete more effectively in a modern career. He envisioned his son living off the reservation. Perhaps he would go into computers, or engineering, or maybe even law enforcement.

But as he watched Tom and the boy, he regretted not having taught him more about his culture, the real culture of his tribe, not the modern-day dilemmas of poverty, alcoholism, and lack of purpose that John worked with every day. JR needed to know how his people lived before the reservations. He needed to feel the spiritual awareness that came alive when man was one with his surroundings. For this brief period,

JR was learning such things from the old man, and John was grateful that they had come together.

About three hours into the ride, Sue stopped the search party at the end of a box canyon. She turned to the riders and said, "This is a good place to stop for a while. If my memory is correct the dugout is about a mile or two up that ravine. I'm going to ride ahead and check it out."

"Wait, young one," Crowfeather responded. "You leap into things like a young deer who is blinded by light. Have you noticed the hawk who has followed us these last few miles? Let the hawk fly ahead of you so he can tell you if the man is there. Also, you must mark your path with signs so if you do not return, we can follow your trail. And that striped coat, you should take it off. Put on your brown bedroll blanket so that no one can see you as the sun shines on the hills. Remember that the meadowlark says this is a dangerous man. You must be on guard."

Sue slowly dismounted from her horse. She wasn't used to taking orders, nor was she accustomed to being reprimanded for her judgment. But she knew Tom was right. She had been too eager to ride ahead without preparation. Removing her bedroll from the saddle, Sue gathered the wool blanket and wrapped it around her shoulders. JR pulled a blue bandanna from his pocket and began cutting it into strips.

"Here," he said handing her the pieces of blue cloth. "You can use these to mark your path."

"Thanks, JR," Sue said, taking the strips and placing them through her belt loops. "Why don't you ride with me a while. Then you can take care of my horse when we get closer to the place. I want to crawl in for a closer look when we find the hideout."

A short time later, the two riders rode up the steep banks of the canyon and headed north. They tied the bandanna strips on clumps of sagebrush to mark their path. As Tom had predicted, the hawk remained with them, flying ahead about a quarter mile, then circling back to the riders. After riding for about 30 minutes, they noticed that the hawk had not returned from its last outing. Sue pulled her binoculars from the case and scanned the sky, searching for signs of the bird. Finally, she spotted it in the northeastern sky. The hawk was flying in a tight circle, soaring upward and then diving, repeating the cycle again and again.

"There's the sign," Sue exclaimed. "The hawk has found something. I'm going in on foot now. I'll be back as soon as I can see if anyone is out there."

In a crouched position, Sue began to move in the direction of the hawk. Soon she was positioned just beneath the hawks' flight pattern. Lowering her body closer to the ground, she moved cautiously forward until, quite by accident, she was almost atop the structure. The dugout was as she had remembered it, set into the side of the hill. The front door, made of rough planks, was closed. Next to the door was a small opening that once was a window. The remainder of the structure was underground. Sue saw no signs of activity in the dugout, but as she widened the area of focus she spotted a pile of fresh horse manure at the side of the entrance. She thought of the old story of the boy who was an optimist, 'If there's horse shit, then there must be a pony!' Broadening her search of the site, Sue began to look for the animal. There, about 300 yards below, staked in a small patch of grass, was the horse, a sandy-colored Appaloosa. Suddenly she heard a scream overhead. The hawk, still circling, shrieked as it soared and plummeted above her. Glancing back to the house, Sue saw a man standing at the door. She crouched lower into the grass and watched as the man gazed up at the hawk, then turned and retreated through the doorway.

"Well, we've found him," she thought, "but we're going to play hell getting him out of there. The place is like a fortress, with no way in except the front door. And he's got a good view of everything around him."

Sue cautiously moved away from the hideout and walked back to JR and the horses. Explaining that she had found the dugout and, in fact, Sam Pickens was secured inside, the two riders returned to the canyon. The hawk continued to fly above them, as if obligated to assure their safety.

"Well, we found him," declared Sue, dismounting from her horse and tying the reins to a nearby patch of sagebrush. "He's in the dugout, and it'll be pretty hard to get him out of there. She picked up a stick and in the dirt, outlined the layout of the site. "He can see everything from here to there," she said pointing to the area surrounding the front of the structure. "We can approach from the north side of the hill, but we will have to wait for him to come out the front door."

The trackers discussed their options. They could position themselves behind the dugout and wait for Pickens to come out. But since it was impossible to get close enough to the structure to grab him, he could easily retreat when he saw them. They could create a diversion, something to draw him down to the area where his horse was staked. They also considered smoking him out of the dugout, using a flare cartridge fired from a 12-gage shotgun. Of course, the final alternative would be to contact the Federal enforcement officers, who would fly in and remove him. They quickly decided against the latter.

After debating whether to wait for Pickens to leave the hideout on his own, or to smoke him out with the flare, it was decided to use the flare. They knew he must be captured quickly, before nightfall, and it was already early afternoon.

Establishing a base camp along the ridge where Sue had sited the dugout, the team prepared to move in and capture Sam Pickens. JR would crawl to a point just above the dugout, positioned to apprehend him from above if he bolted from the front door. Sue would assume a position to the left of the structure, prepared to stop him if he ran towards the horse. Kathryn, armed with her 38, would stand guard at the right. John it was decided, would be the shooter, aiming the shotgun at the window opening to assure that the smoke cartridge would enter the dugout. Tom Crowfeather would stay behind at the camp. As he put it, "I am an old man, better I leave the capture to younger bones. I have much work to do here at the camp."

Kathryn could feel her heart pounding. She had not felt this kind of rush in years. In fact, the last time she remembered this kind of fear mixed with exhilaration was on her sail boat. They were returning from a Miami to Key West race then, when a severe storm bore down on them. The boat pitched and reeled in the water as the crew struggled to reef the sails. Acting too late, the main mast cracked, heaving the mainsail overboard to drag in the water. Only her crew's quick thinking prevented the boat from being dragged under. Grabbing wire cutters, a crewman severed the halyards, allowing the mast and sail to detach from the boat. She was experiencing the same feelings now that she had when they struggled to save the boat, overwhelming apprehension but with sharpened senses and a focus on success.

John, on the other hand, felt a sense of calmness as positioned himself in the tall grass overlooking the front of the dugout. One shot into the open window and the ordeal would be over. Hopefully, Pickens would surrender. They would take him into custody, call the authorities and Sam Pickens would go to trial. A neatly wrapped package, taken care of locally with no fanfare and little publicity. Things would return to normal. He pulled the gun to his shoulder, held it tightly, and fired.

The smoke cartridge hit its mark. Within moments smoke billowed from the window. Each person stood ready to move in as Pickens fled the hideout. Several minutes passed and there were no signs of movement from the hideout. The smoke from the window opening began to dissipate and still no sign of the fugitive. "Damn," thought John, "what if he wasn't in the building?" He scanned the area for signs of movement, knowing that if Pickens had been outside when the shot was fired, there was little chance of spotting him. He had to, somehow, get to the horse and secure it. It would be easier to track Pickens on foot than on horseback.

Kathryn also thought something had gone wrong. She saw no activity from the dugout and wondered what to do next. Reaching in her bag for binoculars, she felt someone grab her throat from behind. "Don't say a word, pretty lady," whispered a voice. "You and I are leaving."

Kate froze, feeling what seemed like a gun barrel pushed against her back. "Now give me the bag," Pickens demanded. She held the bag behind her as he roughly grabbed it from her hand.

"Oh shit," she thought, "can't someone see what's going on here? Please, dear God, do something!" Just then a shot rang out, and Pickens threw her to the ground. He pulled her behind a large stand of sagebrush, and grabbing her by the hair turned her face to his.

"Your going to tell them if I hear one more shot, I'm going to hurt you, not kill you, just hurt you real bad. Understand?"

"Yes," she stammered.

"Now do it! And tell them we are going to walk down to my horse. If they try to shoot me, then you are going down with me."

Kate cried out from the bushes. She warned her friends that she and Sam were moving towards the horse, and any move to stop them would be met with certain harm to her.

A voice replied, "Just stay calm, Sam. We won't try to stop you. Just let her go when you get to your horse. We won't follow you if you just let her go."

Pickens lifted her to her feet and grabbed her waste as he again lodged the gun barrel between her shoulders. Kathryn took a lead from John's words and gently said, "Look, Sam, we both want to get out of here safely. Just stay calm. I'll do everything you ask, and we'll walk out of here together." She felt the gunbarrel ease slightly from her back. They began to walk down the hill.

Sue, JR, and John were stunned by the site of Pickens and his hostage cautiously making their way towards the meadow below. Each felt helpless, but knew that any move might trigger an explosive reaction from the man. They could only hope that old Tom had seen them from his position on the ridge and would go for help.

Pickens quickened the pace as they were midway down the hill. He angrily jided the women as they descended. "You folks had to be pretty stupid if you thought I only had one exit from that cave! You think I didn't plan what would happen if I had to get away? That may look like a hole in the ground but I had all the comforts of home, honey, and that included a telephone and a back door. I'm walking out a here, and you're comin' with me!"

As they approached the horse, Kathryn knew that there was little chance of her being released. Sam would need her as protection. She began to look for an opportunity to break away from his grasp. Were it not for the gun, she thought she may be able to overpower him. Perhaps he would be distracted as he took his horse from the lead rope. However, grabbing the horse's line, he commanded her to lay face down on the ground. Releasing the end of the tether, he left one end of it attached to the horse and with the other end, he tied Kathryn's hands securely behind her back. "You better hope that ol' horse don't bolt," he sneered, "'cause you're going with him if he does! We're just gonna walk out a here nice an' easy." With Kathryn now secured by both Pickens and the horse, they retreated from the meadow.

When John saw the rope tied around Kate's hands, he knew there was no chance of her being released. He had to get back to the campsite and try to summon help. He hoped that Kathryn had left her cell phone at the camp. If not, it would be a long ride back to civilization.

Back at the camp, the old man was no where around. John called to him, but got no response. Just then, Sue and JR came into view, climbing over the knoll from the dugout. "Oh. my God, dad," cried JR, "What are we going to do? He took Kate with him, and I think he'll kill her before this is over. Please let me follow them. Maybe I can free her."

"JR, calm down!" his father replied. "No, you're not going to follow them. We don't need two captives out there. Besides we need you to go for help if I can't find Kate's phone." They began searching for the phone in her bedroll and saddlebags.

"I think she took it with her," Sue said. "I seem to remember it being in that bag she was carrying. We need to go get help. By the way, where's Tom?"

John scanned the campsite. "I don't know," he said. "He wasn't here when I got back." Just then JR spotted the old man's horse grazing at the top of the hill. But there was no sign of Tom. "Go up there, JR, and see if you can find him," his father requested.

Sue scanned the ravines below for signs of Pickens and his hostage. She saw nothing. "John," she said. "I think I'd better go for help. I know these badlands, and I'm afraid JR would become lost if he went alone."

"Your right," John answered. "Besides you'll be able to guide the authorities back here."

Sue tightened the cinch on her saddle and was about to mount when JR returned from the hill.

"I can't find Tom anywhere," said the boy. "All that's up there is his horse and his robe, lying on the ground. There's no sign of the old man."

"Damn," responded John, "This a great time for him to disappear. He's probably talking to the spirit guides, but I can't worry about where he is now. We need to start tracking Pickens from a distance. I don't want to leave the old man here, but we'll leave a note explaining what's happened."

Sue left the camp at a full gallop, hoping to find help before nightfall. John and JR decided to create an SOS out of materials left at camp, shirts, blankets, anything that would be visible from the air. All the while they searched the horizon for Tom Crowfeather, hoping he would appear before they had to leave the area. Finally, John began loading his horse with gear: rope, rifle, bedroll, and anything else that he might need to track Pickens and Kate. He was overwhelmed with guilt about the way things had played out. It was his fault that Kathryn had been put in jeprody, his fault that the old man had disappeared. What egotistical ideas had led him to believe that he could lead a frail old man and the people he loved into a situation that endangered their lives. Sam Pickens would have been captured eventually without their assistance. It was his own ego that led him to believe that they could somehow restore the value of old customs and the independent spirit by capturing an evil man. Philosophically it had been a moral deed. Practically, it was an ill conceived and dangerous plan.

Chapter Eighteen

Hostage

Sam Pickens pulled Kathryn to the ground and wrapped the rope that secured both she and the Appaloosa around the trunk of a small cedar tree. "Its time to rest for a while," he said as he removed his left boot to relieve pressure from the blister that was forming on his heel. "Little lady," he continued, "I'm sure glad it was you that I brought along. You're the big-city bitch that got me into this predicament. If you hadn't come out here tryin' to solve that Indian's problem, we would've had that dinosaur packaged and delivered and nobody would have been the wiser. Now I've probably lost my ranch and my family. Hell, I'll be lucky if I can just get out of the country with the money! None of this would have happened if it wasn't for you."

Hearing those comments, Kathryn felt certain that her chances of surviving her capture were diminishing. This was a man who was frightened and angry. And his anger was not diffused; it was focused directly on her. Drawing upon everything she had learned about hostage situations, she began to rehearse her words and actions. She must remain acquiescent, yet not overly submissive. She must continue to engage him in rational conversation. She must not give him reason to panic, she must..., she must... — terrifying thoughts began to race through her mind. Stop! she demanded of her mind. Calmness and clarity must replace panic. John may have been right about her loosing part of her soul in the city, but she hadn't lost the instinct for survival. She was determined to walk out of these badlands and would use anything available to her to save her life.

"Sam, I'm sorry," she said. "I'm sorry you think that I got you into this. Truthfully, you weren't high on our suspect list until Rodney Rassmussen spoke to us. And the way he described it, you didn't really mean to kill Johnson. It was an accident, and I believe that's manslaughter, not murder."

"No, I didn't mean to kill him, I just hit him too hard! But its too late to explain that now," he replied.

Good, said Kate to herself, keep up the rational thought. She continued, "Sam, its not too late. You have a wife and family to support you. You've always made good decisions in the past. Those things are certainly in your favor."

The man was silent, looking out over the prairie. He seemed for a moment to have connected with her words, contemplating all that he was giving away in his frenzied attempt to escape. He remembered how, as a poor farm boy in Oklahoma, he had dreamed about becoming a big rancher with acres of land, fine livestock, and a man who people in the community looked up to and respected. He had worked hard to achieve his dream. It finally became a reality when he married the daughter of a wealthy Oklahoma rancher, and his father-in-law staked him to his first cattle operation. He had struggled to make it successful, and it was by local standards. But Sam had always felt inadequate, never quite measuring up to his father-in-law. That was why, in the mid-90s, he had pulled up roots and resettled his family in South Dakota. The opportunity to raise the finest pure-bred horses in the country would bring him the esteem and fortune he was seeking. But it was the lure of big money that had brought him where he was today, a fugitive running from authorities and about destroy every bit of the life he had built. If only he had walked away from Mark Phip's get-rich proposition. Things would have been so different had he not been seduced into thinking the scheme would work.

Abruptly, Pickens got to his feet. "We'll ride from here. We got a ways to go before we get to the spot where the plane is waiting." He lifted Kathryn into the saddle and pulled his body up behind her. They headed deeper into the badlands and further away from any attempt at rescue.

Chapter Nineteen

Transactions

John and JR stayed at the campsite as long as they could. John brought the old man's horse down from the hill and staked it with Kathryn's buckskin and the packhorses. He saw no evidence of Tom on the hilltop, only his robe and a few feathers scattered upon it. He hoped that his old friend would return to camp and wait for them.

The men descended into the meadow below, where they easily picked up the tracks of the horse and footprints of two people. The held the horses at a fast but steady pace, hoping to make up some of the distance between themselves and the fugitive.

Meanwhile, Sue urgently pushed on in the opposite direction of the camp, finally stopping when she reached the river. Her horse needed water and time to rest, but like any athlete, Sue knew that the horse's muscles would begin to cramp if he didn't remain in motion. She had hoped to sight the search helicopter along the way, but was dismayed to hear or see nothing in the distance. There was no alternative but to follow the river back to road and pray that she could summon help before dark.

Not knowing about the saga being played out deep in the badlands, the search helicopter had returned to Rapid City for fuel. The men on board were frustrated in their efforts. They had searched for two days and had found not so much as a clue as to the whereabouts of Pickens. They planned to make one more run into the area today, then resume the search in the morning. The helicopter was thoroughly covering the area in a grid fashion, flying sector by sector. Only the northwest region remained, and when they were finished there, they could either repeat the grid sequence or halt the search.

Mark Uses-Knives had spent the day in Rapid City, helping to coordinate the exchange of the fossil remains between Dan Fromm and Warren Phips. Fromm had met with the fossil hunter, and agreed to pay $1.2 million for the Triceratops, providing he could examine and authenticate the specimen. Phips had agreed to the terms, but had initially demanded that Fromm accompany him to the Montana site where, according to him, the dinosaur had been discovered. Fromm refused, insisting that the fossil be delivered to the School of Mines Geology Department where he could perform the tests required to authenticate it. Phips, of course, was in no position to bargain. He agreed to the terms, providing Fromm's organization would deposit earnest money in Phips' account, confirming the agreement.

The Bureau hesitated in turning over funds before they had possession of the skeleton, but agreed after a plan had been established to follow Phips to Montana, and locate and secure that site. Phips would transport the bones back to Rapid City, where authorities were prepared to confiscate them.

Warren Phips was not pleased with the time it was taking to complete the transaction. He knew, however, that Fromm was an expert in his craft, and that the authentication process must be completed if the sale were to occur. Knowing that Sam Pickens was securely hidden away, Phips believed there would be more than enough time for the inspection and money transfer. A telephone call that afternoon, however, brought a sense of urgency to the plan. Pickens' hideout had been discovered by a local Indian team who were determined to bring him to justice for the murder of Wes Johnson! Sam demanded that Phips fly into the badlands and take him to safety. Phips didn't know that the situation had escalated, that Pickens had taken a hostage and quite possibly was contemplating another murder.

Warren Phips often cursed the day that he had hooked up with Sam Pickens. When they had planned the operation, almost a year ago, it had seemed entirely feasible. The excavation operation had run smoothly until the appearance of the sheep herder. Pickens death blow to Wesley Johnson made it clear to the fossil hunter that he was dealing with a dangerously unpredictable man. Moreover, Sam's poor judgment in the incident's cover-up, led Phips to believe that the entire project was at risk. The transport and sale of illegal antiquities was one thing, but murder and conspiracy was a entirely new element that Warren Phips wanted no part of. He was, however, left in an untenable position. He had been present at the murder, and Picken's used that fact to push him further into the conspiracy.

Now Phips must make a decision to either assist in Picken's escape, or halt the madness by turning himself in. As he considered the options, a third alternative came to mind. What if Sam Pickens just disappeared in the Badlands? Perhaps someone would find him later, and the authorities, having already cited him for murder, would close the case. Phips then would be free to take all of the proceeds from the sale and walk away from situation a free man. Phips was, of course, unaware that he was already implicated in the scheme and within days would unwittingly hand over both himself and the dinosaur to Federal authorities.

Warren Phips contemplated the last alternative. If he didn't fly in to rescue Pickens, the rancher may wander around in the area until he succumbed to the harsh environment. But he knew that Sam was probably too savvy to allow himself to die out there. He would find a way to turn himself in if it came to that. There also was a question as to whether the Indian party would continue to track him. If they captured him, there was no doubt in Phips' mind that he would be implicated. If Sam Pickens were captured, he would take everyone involved with him. No, if Sam were to disappear in the badlands, he, Phips, would have to aid in the disappearance.

Warren Phips finally decided that the safest way to take care of Sam Pickens, was to assure that he never came out of hiding. He would fly in to the prearranged landing site, subdue Pickens, load him into the airplane, and then drop him somewhere between Faith and Rapid City. It would be months, maybe even years, before anyone found the body. By that time, he would be deep in Costa Rica, tending bananas and collecting Indian artifacts. Warren Phips breathed a sigh of relief as he envisioned the end of his ordeal.

Chapter Twenty

Eagle's Flight

Indian lore has it that man may call upon the animals to help them in times of danger. Man also gains great strength and insight from the "four-leggeds"; fearlessness of the bear, tenacity of the badger, sacred wisdom of the buffalo, and vision of the eagle. Additionally, it has been recorded, that in times of great spiritual crisis, man may be transformed into the animal, thereby acquiring its sacred power, strength, and wisdom. Which of the sacred principals manifested on that crucial day in the badlands of South Dakota, no one knows for sure. Those Native Americans who heard the story and knew Tom Crowfeather have differing opinions. Some say Tom called upon the "four-leggeds" to find his friend, Kathryn, and rescue her from her captor. Others believe it was the old man, himself, who through the miracle of transformation, protected the woman. All will say with certainty, however, that the spiritual powers of the old shaman were responsible for the events that occurred that day.

Sam Pickens and his hostage had arrived at the designated landing strip at about 4:00 pm. They awaited the arrival of Warren Phips and the airplane that was to take Pickens away. At that point, Sam remained uncertain about what to do with Kathryn Stafford. His anger with her had diminished, but she continued to be a threat to his plans for escape. He could kill her now, and leave her body behind. But something in the man's pathos made a distinction between the accidental death of Wesley

Johnson and the cold-blooded murder of this woman. His conscience would not allow him to take another life. So, he decided, he would take her with them, and perhaps drop her off in a desolate area of another state. By the time she was found, they would have made their getaway.

Kathryn was becoming restless as she sat on the hard ground, bound by the rope that held her ankles and wrists together behind her back. It was beginning to get cold and she could feel the circulation draining from her extremities. If there were a rescue underway, it must happen within the next hour, she reasoned. She tried to no avail to loosed the ropes that bound her. And she heard no sounds of approaching helicopters or airplane, only the blustering of the cold north wind.

Sam Pickens stood next to his horse and was beginning to loosen the saddle. As he reached for the cinch, a scream echoed from the heavens, and a huge bird plunged downward. Talons outstretched, the eagle crashed into Pickens, tossing him to the ground. His horse reared and cried out in terror as the bird's talons sunk into the man's back, tearing off his shirt to expose the bloodied shoulders. Helplessly, Sam cried in pain as he flailed his arms to fend off the attacker. But the eagle then grabbed his throat, tearing it open as it would any of its prey. As Kathryn watched in horror, the bird stood upon the motionless body, looking down upon it as if deciding whether to carry it away or stand guard over it. Kathryn desperately struggled to free the ropes from her hands, unsure of the eagle's next movement. The bird stood perfectly still atop the man's chest. Blood spurted from the wound, but the eagle made no attempt to continue the attack. It quietly moved its head to stare at Kathryn. She saw no fear or anger in its eyes, only a curious stare.

Suddenly, Kathryn believed she heard the pounding sound of a helicopter in the distance. Uncertain as to whether she was hallucinating, she looked up into the sky. The eagle, too, must have heard the sound, and he cocked his head upward, looking for the source. Then, as quickly as it had plummeted from the sky, the eagle spread its wings and lifted its body upward, soaring into the distance.

The sound of the helicopter was deafening as lowered to the ground. Two men in silver flight suits emmerged from the craft. They were followed by Sue Badger and Dan Fromm. As the flight crew attended to lifeless body of Sam Pickens, Dan and Sue hovered over Kathryn, untying her restraints and wrapping her in a blanket.

"Kathryn, are you all right?" asked Dan.

"Yes, just cold and exhausted," she replied. "What are you doing here?"

"I was with Uses-Knives in Rapid City when Sue's call came in, and I just had to come along when I heard that he had you out here. You're sure your OK?" Dan had been extremely serious when he had said that he wanted Kathryn in his life. This incident confirmed his feelings. He had strong armed his way on to the helicopter, determined that he would be there when they found her.

Kathryn wrapped her arms around him, holding his warm body close to hers. "Thank you for being here," she said quietly, "Just now you hold a very special place in my heart." Looking up at Sue, Kathryn smiled. "So you were the one who went for help. Boy, have you had a rough day!"

Just then, a small plane approached the site. Flying at an extremely low altitude, it passed overhead but did not land. They watched as it turned westward and disappeared.

"So what the hell happened here?" Sue asked. "Who did this to Pickens?"

"An eagle attacked him," replied Kathryn, and the two women's eyes connected, both understanding the true meaning of the incident.

"Out here, anything can happen," said Sue. "There are powerful forces at work in the badlands."

"Sue," said Kathryn, "I don't want to go back tonight. I want to return to the campsite. I need to be out here just now. Will you come with me?"

"Well, if you're sure you're up to it. I feel the same. I think there's some unfinished business we need to take care of."

Dan Fromm had moved to the suited men who were working over Sam's body. "How is he?", he inquired.

"I'm afraid he's lost too much blood," the crewman replied. "We've got to get him out of here immediately!"

While they were preparing Pickens for transport, two horsemen galloped on to the scene. John and JR had followed the helicopter's flight and arrived just in time to see the stretcher being loaded into the aircraft.

"We've got to leave now," said the pilot. "Do you need help getting in, mam?"

"No," replied Kathryn, relieved that John had arrived. "I'll be staying at out our camp tonight. These men will take me there."

Sue added, "I'm staying too. We'll take good care of her. Tell Mark Uses-Knives we'll be back in Dupree tomorrow."

Dan looked at the women dumbfounded. "Kathryn, if you're staying, can I come with you?"

"No, Dan. Please go back to Rapid with them. There are some things we need do at the camp, just for closure. I'll see you tomorrow, promise." Kathryn gently kissed his lips. "Go, now, my dear man."

Reluctantly, Dan boarded the waiting helicopter. The door slid closed as the craft lifted off, headed for Rapid City. Sue and Kate lifted themselves onto the backs of the men's horses, anxious to share the extraordinary events of the afternoon with their comrades.

Chapter Twenty-One

The Legacy

It was well after sunset when the riders arrived at the camp. At once, they saw the body of the old man, wrapped in his robe. He had made no effort to set up camp or to start a fire, and in the darkness his still body looked gray and lifeless. John quickly jumped from his horse and leaned over Tom.

"He's breathing," said John, "but its very shallow. Quick, build a fire, and lets see if we can't get him warm."

JR began unloading the camp equipment, searching for blankets and the Duralogs they had packed. Kate and Sue scrambled through the brush, looking for anything that would burn. They gathered dry sagebrush and grass. That along with the wood from the camp stools and the wooden boxes used to pack the equipment should provide sufficient heat through the night.

They heated water over the fire, and Sue placed the opened cans of beef stew in the coals to warm. John held the old man, rubbing his weathered hands and speaking to him in his native tongue. Tom slowly opened his eyes and whispered, "I am very tired. Let me sleep now."

"Soon Tom, but first you must drink and eat," said John.

"Take my pipe from the bag," said Crowfeather, "you must smoke it and thank the spirits for all that has happened today. The pipe will bring the strength we need to survive the night."

As soon as the camp had been set up and they had warmed their stomachs with stew and hot coffee, everyone gathered around the old one. With renewed energy, Crowfeather took the pipe in his fragile hands and lifted it to the sky. They each took a puff of smoke, thanking God for their safe return. When the ceremony was completed, Tom spoke. "I must talk to you tonight about important things, things that you will carry with you for all of your lives. I am a man who was given strong *wankan* power. I have used it wisely and with great respect. But I fear that the younger generations no nothing about these powers, and those that do use it selfishly to profit from the curiosity of the white man. Tonight you will each be filled with the powers of *wankan tanka*, and depending upon your level of consciousness and experience, you will use these powers to benefit our people."

The old man of the Wolf Clan watched his friends and could see that they were ready to hear what he had to say. "Sue Badger," he started, "you are the one who will carry on my connection with the animal spirits. Ever since you were a little girl, you spoke to and understood the animals. Now you must connect with them more closely. You shall have the spirit power of the animals, especially the wolf. You must learn the ways of the wolf and practice them in all that you do. Your gifts will strengthen as you use them, and you will discover that you have the power to heal those around you who believe."

Sue remained silent, only acknowledging that she understood what he had said.

Crowfeather continued. "John Redbull, you are a voice of your people. You must begin to live your life in the old ways so that you can teach others. You are respected by the tribe and you must use that respect to bring knowledge and health to them. Our people did not drink alcohol like my sons do today. They worked to provide for their families and to help the tribal community. They shared with one another and they respected their elders. You must teach them to do so again. If you practice the *wankan* powers, the spirits will guide your work."

They waited for Tom to continue, watching as his strength diminished, and his voice became a whisper.

"My young one," he said, looking at JR, "you are just beginning your journey of life. You must do the vision quest and the Sundance. You will work with your father to help the people. You and your father must become close, as one. Together you will study the old ways and help each other to learn. He has forgotten many of the old things, and you have never known them, so, in a way, you are both just beginning to walk the path. Listen with your ears, your eyes, and your heart and you will gain wisdom and *wankan* power. You live in a world where pictures move through the sky and machines think like men. The spirit powers will teach you to hold man and God in high esteem and to not worship the machines over the spirit of humans and nature."

"And finally you, my young friend," he turned to Kathryn and continued, "you are not one of our people, but you and your father were always held in high regard. Your father always met us with respect and you learned well from him. You too must study the old ways and live your life according to the ways of nature. If you remain disconnected with Mother Earth, your soul becomes empty. If you fill it with the songs of birds and the breath of the wind you will once again find purpose and beauty on the earth. You must also come to a meeting with the souls of your father and mother. They should know that you live your life in the reflection of their teachings. And one last thing, my little one, you will take my young horse, Shania, and keep her with you. She is my gift to you for allowing this old man to ride with you and meet with the spirit guides one last time. Find time in your busy world to love this horse. She will bring you joy and free you from the burden of your work. It is difficult sometimes for you to see the good things our creator has put on earth. In your job you see only the ugly things men do to one another."

"Thank you, Tom," said Kathryn, the tears welling in her eyes. "I will never forget this trip. I know it was you who saved my life today, and now you have given it purpose."

Crowfeather smiled and said, "I am very tired now. We must sleep so we can go home in the morning."

Tom Crowfeather died in his sleep that night. He died on a hilltop, wrapped in his woolen robe, much the same as his ancestors did many years ago. They had wanted to leave him there, to rest on a pole platform as was done in the old days. They knew, however, that they must carry him home. His soul would remain in these hills, they were sure, cared for by animals he loved.

Chapter Twenty-Two

Farewell

The Rapid City airport was filled with warmth and sadness as Kathryn awaited Northwest Flight 4755. John and his wife, JR, Sue, and Dan Fromm waited with her at the gate. Kathryn assured them all that she would return in August to begin preparations for her prairie cabin. Sue promised to care for her horse, Shania Twain, and JR gave her his commitment to visit her in the summer and to begin looking into programs offering degrees in law enforcement or computers. John could only stand at the window, gazing over the tarmac. Good-byes weren't easy for him; the words were just never there.

Dan Fromm would be returning to Pennsylvania in a few weeks, and from there, would fly to Miami for a visit. He had already loaded up on books from Prairies Edge, hoping to better understand what had happened to Sam Pickens and the Indian search party that afternoon in the badlands.

Sam Pickens never recovered from the eagle's attack. He died the following day at the Rapid City Medical Center. Warren Phips was arrested when he returned from Montana with the Triceratops. No one ever knew what he had planned for Sam Pickens the day he flew over the helicopter landing site in the badlands. As it turned out, nature prevailed, so Warren Phips never had the opportunity to add murder to the long list of criminal and civil charges against him.

The Triceratops arrived intact at the South Dakota School of Mines

& Technology. It would be held there until after the trial. Then hopefully the prehistoric creature would be assembled somewhere so that people might study it and learn about the times before man, when dinosaurs, the first 'four-leggeds", roamed the earth.

****